About the Author

Aalia is a progressive activist and philosophy major.

Birth Of Nero

Utsav

Birth Of Nero

Olympia Publishers
London

www.olympiapublishers.com
OLYMPIA PAPERBACK EDITION

Copyright © Utsav 2023

The right of Utsav to be identified as author of
this work has been asserted in accordance with sections 77 and 78
of the Copyright, Designs and Patents Act 1988.

All Rights Reserved

No reproduction, copy or transmission of this publication
may be made without written permission.
No paragraph of this publication may be reproduced,
copied or transmitted save with the written permission of the
publisher, or in accordance with the provisions
of the Copyright Act 1956 (as amended).

Any person who commits any unauthorized act in relation to
this publication may be liable to criminal
prosecution and civil claims for damage.

A CIP catalogue record for this title is
available from the British Library.

ISBN: 978-1-80439-477-9

This is a work of fiction.
Names, characters, places and incidents originate from the writer's
imagination. Any resemblance to actual persons, living or dead, is
purely coincidental.

First Published in 2023

Olympia Publishers
Tallis House
2 Tallis Street
London
EC4Y 0AB

Printed in Great Britain

Dedication

Dedicated to the trans community.

"What a piece of work is a man. How noble in reason, how infinite in faculties, in form and moving how express and admirable, in action how like an angel, in apprehension how like a god: the beauty of the world, the paragon of animals! And yet to me what is this quintessence of dust?"

-William Shakespeare

Part I

Just Another Day...
It was the first day of Junior year at Clairemont High School, and lunch had begun. Joshua sat down at an empty table, in his typical grumpy and dissatisfied mood. He had endured two excruciating hours listening to his English and Physics teachers drone on about class rules and instructions, and now it was time to eat the crummy sandwich his grandmother made him. It was quite loud in the cafeteria, Children chattering away about their summers, sports teams, video games, whatever else normies found interesting.

Of course, nobody would sit near Joshua's table, the three additional seats remaining empty.

There was a general feeling of either contempt or indifference at the sight of Joshua amongst the kids in Clairemont High School, and amongst the community in general for that matter. It wasn't because Joshua did anything particularly reprehensible or eyebrow raising for that matter... it was more so that he existed.

The town of Clairemont was a rather small subsection of the central urban center of Chataluma. Despite its close proximity in distance its character was fundamentally different. While Chataluma was a loud, raunchy, vibrant city with all sorts of peculiar individuals and cultures, Clairemont could essentially be described as a small church community. There wasn't an enforced mechanism for theocracy, however virtually everyone attended Church, gathered together for holidays and events while treating the community as absolute in value. There were well defined cultural norms regarding the type of clothes one wears, the activities they can appropriately participate in, and the essence of how one must conduct themselves.

Unfortunately, Joshua was seen as an anathema to all these sacrosanct communal values.

Joshua, however, couldn't reasonably be the first to blame for the way he was perceived amongst others. His father was a worthless drunkard living off the community pension system. He stood isolated from the rest of the community, never going out for weekly church gatherings, community meetups, or really anything for that matter. There was a feeling of contempt permeating throughout the community around Joshua's father and it would be a mark on him from the moment he stepped onto school. The gossip and rumors about him that circulated in a vacuum ranged from silly and frivolous to downright troublesome. "Satanic," "Pedophile," "Waste of space" were just a few that were often casually thrown out there.

Of course, Joshua saw a dimension of his father that many couldn't, and it wasn't a pleasant or wholesome one. It was raw, impersonal, real. Every beating, every scar. There wasn't often even a justification, Joshua merely hovered around as an omnipresent punching bag to satisfy his father's sickening urges. Joshua never fully understood how his own father could treat him in such a hostile, brutish way, the entire situation felt like an enigma. Of course, there was no place to run or hide, his father was basically the only family he ever had. Well there was also his grandmother. But she stayed permanently in the Clairemont Hospital, three miles from where Joshua and his father lived.

Joshua would ride his bike to his grandmother every morning where she'd have his lunch made for him. How she managed to have the willpower and strength to complete that task every school day was beyond comprehension to Joshua, but he felt a strangely intimate connection with his grandmother despite her seldom interacting or speaking to him. How could she? She was beyond incapacitated, her vocal cords effectively powerless and her ligaments crushed to the point where all movement rendered a degree of pain to the rest of the body that was simply incomprehensible.

And yet, this broken-down woman would have ready at her disposal Joshua's lunch for the school day. It wasn't a particularly high-quality meal or something worth savoring but it was food and given her physical state it was vigorous and praiseworthy effort. Effort his father couldn't emulate one to tenth of Joshua would often visit his grandmother, and sit by her in the hospital ward, in a state of tranquility. He could feel his grandmother's calm vibrancy radiating from the hospital room and beyond even with the lack of speech. It wasn't ideal but knowing somebody even remotely cared about the plights that Joshua faced truly infused a certain vitality to everything Joshua did, a feeling of strength.

Wanting to make his grandmother proud was the underlying justification Joshua internalized for himself to even keep his cool with the douchebags he had to endure every school day, the useless assignments he had to complete, the irritating irrationality he had to reconcile with amongst the school staff.

And that was no easy task to say the least Joshua may have had his reputation tainted by his father, but it wasn't exactly difficult for kids at Clairemont High to pick on him. His slouched walk, clumsy antics, and queer demeanor certainly made him a punching bag for his peers. His messy, black hair deprived of a hairline, the broken glasses he wore around in public, and his shirts with displays of various colorful anime characters certainly wasn't a fashion statement that went unnoticed.

Joshua would often hear snickers along with amused gazes as he moved through the halls of Clairemont High School, and occasionally felt light to moderate shoves from behind while heading towards his destinations, often in front of school staff who simply looked aside. It was general consensus amongst his peer and the staff that Joshua was a degenerate homosexual, some going as far as to see him as a manifestation of the demonic. Joshua never understood this sentiment, because he never particularly found men to be sexually arousing.

But that didn't prevent the onslaught of jokes, memes and mockery which constantly surrounded Joshua and his supposedly homosexual predilections. The way he spoke, his hand gestures, his clothing, everything was put under intense oversight and produced endless vapid speculations. However, truth be told, Joshua had an intense longing and attraction towards the aesthetics and ideals of the feminine.

Joshua would often privately visit the nearby community mall, to try on exotic dresses, and various feminine assortments of clothing. He would enter the fitting room and twirl around in a dress, gazing at himself in the mirror, sometimes tearing up without even understanding why. He knew something was deeply wrong with him, in fact he couldn't even comprehend how some people would react to how he spent his spare time if they ever found out.

Joshua even masturbated at the prospect of appearing

feminine, and cross dressing. He couldn't grasp what it was or what it meant, but he knew he wasn't gay. Regardless of how vigorously Joshua's community wanted him to internalize the idea of his homosexual degeneracy and despite how much they wanted him to come forth and beg for repentance like a sheep, he knew it was something else, something he couldn't truly pinpoint.

***

As Joshua bitterly bit into his stale sandwich, the bell rang, marking the end of the lunch period. Joshua threw away the sandwich he had eaten a quarter of, and half consciously gazed at the swarm of children exiting the cafeteria to the halls. With a deep sigh, he began to join them. The feeling of dread had subconsciously entered Joshua's mind, the realization that it would be another year of pure emptiness, and misery. Joshua walked along the narrow hallway corridors to his third period class, European history taught by Mr. Hudson. As Joshua begrudgingly entered the room, he suddenly froze. A magnificent painting stood in front of him. It depicted the shadow of a man playing a Cithara gazing at the sight of brilliant flames burning through an ancient Roman city. Joshua was so immersed by the portrait; the nearby snickers weren't even audible to him.

Joshua often felt the visceral urge to scream "fuck you" to every "human being" surrounding his god forsaken life, to topple every chair and table around him, to flip off every individual who plagued his miserable life, soulless Cretans with no regard for what he felt and experienced and went through. He wanted to run into the small forest which surrounded the town and whimper in misery, in exile, liberated from the coercive traditions and the sheep who flock to reaffirm them. But there was something unique to this portrait, an almost subtle and majestic form of destruction, in a sinister way perhaps even a romantic aura. The man wasn't raging, he gracefully played his instrument as he reveled at the destruction of Rome. Joshua knew he shouldn't feel the gut emotions he was feeling, knew they were distasteful, but he couldn't help himself. How many more times was he gonna be called a faggot? How many more times was he gonna be shoved around like an inanimate object? But killing? Ravaging entire communities?

Clearly what the painting depicted was vile...

A relatively elderly and wrinkled man with large spectacles approached where Joshua stood, breaking his trance. "It's a lovely painting, isn't it?" Joshua gazed into the man's pitch-black eyes. The elderly man looked at the painting with a smile. "Some say Nero will return to bless us one day "Anyways young man, take a seat, we have class to attend to!" The rest of the class period was a snooze like the preceding ones, as the teacher droned on about class expectations and rules but the image of the man playing the fiddle as Rome burnt to ashes wouldn't dissipate from Joshua's mind. As class concluded, Joshua shrugged off the thoughts and headed out for his final class period, but he couldn't help noticing the way the elderly man gazed at him, as if he was penetrating his soul.

Joshua headed up the long stairway for his final period when he noticed someone that suddenly gave him an immense shudder. There stood Maximillian P. Wallace, the most feared and vicious kid in the entire school. He was seven feet tall, with lengthy shoulders, Hawaiian shorts and a collared t-shirt. He often instigated fights, spread rumors, and stirred chaos at school, and he did so with near absolute impunity. His father, Robert Wallace, was a wealthy tech mogul who funded a significant amount of the town's infrastructure and had significant connections to virtually every aspect of the school. He was blessed by the town's local church with many rewards and honors for his "incredible work with philanthropy."

Maximillian went up the staircase chatting away with two of his friends, moving at a visibly slow pace which was clearly irritating those behind him. Joshua gazed up at him, suddenly realizing that the tingling sensation of fear had manifested into pure hatred. The way he shoved everyone around in school, most often of all Joshua, the way he would senselessly spread the crudest of rumors without the slightest sentiment of shame almost made Joshua envious. For it must've truly felt liberating and powerful to be untethered from any conscience.

At that moment however something truly out of the ordinary occurred. A small boy, with short black hair, pale skin and an empty expression of nihilistic solitude in his light brown eyes gently nudged Maximillian aside to move upstairs. And what ensued subsequently was unmitigated pandemonium. Maximillian gave a loud hollower, as if he had been brutally struck by a spear and grabbed the child who made the light nudge by the collar of his shirt. Suddenly everyone near the proximity of the staircase looked away from what they were doing to examine the situation.

Joshua looked into the young boy's eyes, which suddenly appeared petrified. Joshua's first instinct was to stand by and allow the disproportionate retribution to take its course. He didn't want disarray and chaos this early into the school year but after a moment's hesitation, in a split-second Joshua did the unthinkable. As Maximillian had put up his fist, ready to strike a blow at the confused child, Joshua pushed the people around him aside and lunged at Maximillian's feet. Maximillian collapsed but quickly grabbed onto the staircase railing to prevent tumbling down, but the force of his collapse sent his friends stumbling down the stairs, taking everyone behind with them.

To further exacerbate the situation Joshua grabbed a pencil from his pocket and stabbed Maximillian's hand which held onto the railway. Maximillian screamed in agony and tripped down the flight of stairs, joining the other bodies which inadvertently fell down the stairs during the process of events. The young boy looked up at Joshua with tears streaming down from his eyes and suddenly leaped at him to give a hug. Joshua awkwardly stood there and patted his head.

The students who hadn't fallen down the stairs scrambled from the area. Joshua noticed the principal arriving at the scene with the school security officer next to him. He gently pushed the young boy off of him, tears visibly continuing to stream from his eyes. The boy shuddered but Joshua grabbed his hand. "Be safe." The boy looked into Joshua's eyes with a light smile emanating from an otherwise tormented face. Joshua swiftly smiled back and realizing the serious predicament he was in, rushed up the remaining flight of stairs.

The situation seemed inescapable, there were going to be police reinforcements any minute now and there would be people waiting downstairs to capture him if he took the elevator closest to the exit. Suddenly a light bulb moment struck in Joshua's head. It was an insane plan, but it was the only option. Joshua pulled the fire alarm near the proximity of where he stood and rushed to the other side of the top floor and scurried down a flight of stairs, which led to a door out of the building at the far-right side of the school. Joshua pushed through the mass of students attempting to escape the building as the fire alarm continued to holler and arriving at the first floor of the building, lunged for the door out of the school but as he reached for the door, an arm grabbed him from behind. There stood the school security guard, a foreboding and powerful presence whose grasp on Joshua's arms produced an intense jolt of pain throughout his body.

Luckily Joshua had prepared for this precise intervention, and in a split-second spit on the security guard's face, swiftly pulled his arms away from the man's firm grip and grabbed the fire hydrant next to the door. Before the guard could even lift his finger, Joshua pulled the pin of the extinguisher, and aiming at the guard squeezed the lever, the water blasting the man to the floor. Joshua threw the extinguisher at the man and dashed out the door. There were already cops occupying the front and back of the school building and two of them departed from their post to head towards the side of the building. Joshua darted towards the forest twenty feet from where he stood, the officers a few feet away, and before he knew it his environment had transformed into a lush forest habitat, and suddenly he stood surrounded by pine trees, lengthy grass and a variety of different flowers, the sun barely penetrating the thick branches.

Birth

Robert P. Wallace gazed at his wounded son as his agonizing screams of contempt filled the air, his body grimacing as the stretcher took him away into the ambulance. Clenching his fist tightly, a sudden sensation was emanating from Mr. Wallace, a feeling he had seldom experienced. Guilt. It was clearly his fault that his son was in this current predicament. He had enabled his son's abusive and foolish behavior from the very beginning. Showering him with everything he ever wanted as a child, using his unscrupulous stranglehold over the town as a means to threaten anyone who challenged Maximillians toxic behavior, refusing to infuse a sense of humility into his child's actions.

However, it was too late now to change course. Retribution was necessary if he wanted to save his son from further humiliation and if he wasn't careful potentially death. The ghoulish freak who targeted his poor child would be far simpler to destroy than his typical enemy. The community already perceived him as a malignant threat, eyes and ears would certainly be alert to his whereabouts. The community police utilized all their resources for the specific purpose of finding the child responsible for this grotesque act. To mitigate the challenge further, the boy had one transparent weakness, he had love. Robert's local sources seemed to indicate that Joshua had a very subpar relationship with his father, rather typical of decadent minors; however, according to his sources from Clairemont Hospital, the child had an immense affinity for his grandmother, often visiting her for extensive periods of time. Sometimes, exiting the hospital with tears emanating from his eyes. A subtle, yet sinister smile crawled down Mr. Wallace's face. He didn't have to find the child; Joshua would come to him. Robert swiftly flipped open his phone and began dialing a number. "Mr. Hudson, you know what must be done."

***

Joshua began panting intensely, shaken and bereft of all energy. He had sprinted through the forest for hours, until he was certain that the Clairemont police wouldn't be capable of capturing him. Trees, bushes and flowers populated virtually every inch of the area surrounding him. The forest was known to get thicker as it approached the urban center. Chataluma couldn't be far from here. Joshua slowly collapsed onto the flower bed he was on top of, and suddenly exploded in tears. This was the cost of playing hero. He would now be cast into the position of an outlaw forever, living his life off false identities, constantly attempting to resist capture, never given a moment to breathe. Worst of all, he would most likely never see his poor grandmother again. Yet, what left Joshua truly perplexed was his peculiar lack of empathy. He had left a teenager brutally wounded and potentially in critical conditions, but he was certain he'd do it again if he could.

Maximillian and his father had left an unprecedented reign of terror in their wake, unencumbered by any sense of justice or moral introspection. Somebody had to interject a sense of humility into these depraved creatures, to show that resistance wasn't futile. Of course, Joshua doubted the message would resonate with the people of Clairemont. They would likely consume dog shit if their overlords had asked them to. However, it wasn't merely a statement as much as Joshua would like himself to believe it was. Seeing that child's petrified face up close, as Maximillian was prepared to clobber him with all his might, Joshua felt an intense connection, almost a longing for somebody like him. He was probably just like Joshua. A freak to everyone around him, anathema to their "divine" sensibilities. What the people of Clairemont would declare a "low life." A slight smile emanated from Joshua's face. Freaks have gotta look out for fellow freaks.

As Joshua sat still on the flower bed, lingering in a whirlwind of contemplative thought, something radiating with immense beauty caught his eyes. There, on the edge of the flower bed, stood a beautiful assortment of blue flowers, the leaves dancing with the light winds as the petals glowed. He remembered the exact name of this beautiful flower from his botany class.

They were called the Myosotis Sylvatica or forget me not. Joshua began to creep towards the beautiful plant, his heart pulsating with sudden energy. In a slow and graceful manner Joshua began to touch the flower petals, chills emanating from his spine. But why did this particular flower have such an intense visceral impact on him? He had seen numerous beautiful plants, arguably more extraordinary than this one. Yet, none of them produced such a longing, erotic sensation within him.

Suddenly, without a moment's hesitation, Joshua feverishly pulled the flower from its roots. There, underneath the Myosotis Sylvatica, stood a small red book, covered in dirt. Joshua's eyes began to twinkle with amazement and curiosity as he scraped off the dirt that was all over the cover. As the title of the book became visible, Joshua's heart stopped pounding and his jaw dropped to the floor. **The Diary of Brennan McCarthy.** That was his father's name! But a diary? His father had always just been a drunken fiend. He was deprived of any meaningful qualities. What could this text possibly illuminate? Joshua removed the book from the ground and began to open its pages.

***

April 27, Dear Diary,
I have had to endure my parents screeching at one another all day. Haven't had the opportunity to eat even a portion of a meal. I dare not confront the foreboding presence of my family. I continue to consume reruns of Disney movies,

and they never fail to make me cry like a little child. This thing called love. If only I could experience just a taste of it, if only I didn't have to be all alone as life eviscerates my soul inch by inch.

Joshua looked away for a moment. He had only begun reading, yet a sense of guilt started piercing his heart. He had always seen his father as devoid of humanity or dignity. Yet just a glance into the past contradicted such hasty assumptions. His father was all too human.

Joshua's gentle tears lightly brushed the page, leaving wet smudges across the text. He continued, enamored by his father's words…

March 28, Dear diary,
I met a rather handsome man while working my part time job at the local diner. He had ordered our famous ham sandwich. I'm not particularly sure why I memorized that, I don't typically care about what the customer's order. The moment he walked into our establishment I found myself mystified by his thin yet resoundingly confident physique, short and well parted blonde hair and light green eyes which I struggled to look away from. My feeling of awestruck lust transformed into genuine hopefulness when I noticed him glancing towards my direction as I was cleaning tables. I quickly looked away, but I was suspiciously certain he caught my stare.

Joshua stopped for a moment. He had presumed that reading his father's diary would elucidate a clearer portrait of his ambiguous past, but it had thus far merely exacerbated his confusion.

Was his father sexually interested in another man? He must've changed his mind at some point, Joshua thought. *How else could he have given birth? Furthermore, was this why the citizens of Clairemont felt such vigorous animosity towards his father? Were they familiar with his homosexual proclivities?* Joshua continued reading with intense curiosity and intrigue until a particular entry really struck him.

April 2, Dear Diary,
I feel an intense sense of gratitude for having had the courage to approach Steven last night. He had managed to bring a ladder and sneak into my room today. We began by watching a movie together, his head gently resting on my shoulders. Midway through the film I began bursting out in tears. I felt deeply embarrassed, in fact up till then, I spent all my energy attempting to repress the tears that desired to flow out of my eyes. Steven looked me in the eyes, his expression emanating with concern. I began speaking to him about my family. How they were slowly ripping my soul from my corporeal self.

Constantly taunting me about my inadequacies, insulting me for not being the straight. A student they desired, never approaching me with concern or love for who I was. Words came gushing out of my mouth, I was unaware if they were coherent, but I had to say them.

As I released all the visceral anguish stored inside me for so long, I was half anxious Steven would finally see me for the freak that I was. Regardless, I had to release my pain to somebody, I couldn't shelter it forever. Much to my absolute shock however, a tortured smile emanated from Steven's face. After pausing for a moment, he began to

speak. He delicately whispered five words into my ears, striking me with utter shock. "I wasn't born a man."

The moment he read those words; the journal slipped from Joshua's sweaty fingers. For a moment, he sat still on the forest grounds, feeling a sense of utter revulsion. What utter deviancy. How could a female, someone with a fucking uterus become a man? Was that not an act against nature itself? But Joshua's utter bewilderment was instantly balanced by a hesitant sense of clarity. Did he resemble this "boy?" Was his internal feminine inclinations and desire to express himself as a girl a sign? A sign that he was born in the wrong body. After pausing for a moment, Joshua shook his head. It was all far too overwhelming to ponder upon.

He picked up his father's journal and continued where he left off. His father's reaction to what Steven said however wasn't quite the same as Joshua's.

I stood silent for a moment upon hearing what Steven had told me. But then a smile radiated from my tear-stricken face. "Oh honey, I haven't met a man quite like you before. But you have me hooked!" I giddily exclaimed. Steven was now streaming with tears, but he wasn't in pain. In fact, it looked to me like an expression of relief. "Brennan!" he stated with resolute passion. "If only you'd have raised me instead." For a moment my room was pitch silent. I could hear noise from the downstairs TV emanating from a distance. Must've been baseball or some shit.

A few seconds had passed till I thrusted Steven over to my side and began kissing his lips. He held onto me tight, as I passionately kissed and licked every inch of his sweet face. I had never felt so alive. Moments later we began to

slip onto my bed and decided to have some fun...

Reading the journal entry should've left Joshua wrought with dismay and discomfort but he couldn't help but find himself chuckling. He had never seen his father display even an inkling of joy or amusement in all the time he had spent with him. And yet here he was, presumably at the apex of his life, negating every social norm imaginable to satisfy his primal urges with the love of his life. Joshua was beginning to recognize his father in a way he never thought possible.

Joshua continued reading the diary with utter intrigue and bewilderment until he reached an entry that left him with an unthinkable realization.

June 1, Dear Diary,
Today I have been blessed with such extraordinary news! I'm going to be having a baby! Steven had visited the doctor and he was informed that he was pregnant. Of course, we have done a good job being secretive with our relationship. If the town had found out about the two of us, I wouldn't be stunned if they crucified us! Of course, this pregnancy will make it significantly more difficult to hide our trail, but we'll have to manage. I just hope between the two of us we can find some cash and get out of this hell hole! It's no place fit to raise our baby together.

It was him. It must've been him. Who else could it possibly be? Joshua was the baby they were referring to. But he simply couldn't wrap his head around it. "Blessed with such extraordinary news." If his father was so ecstatic about having a child, why the fuck did he treat Joshua with such disdain and animosity? The scars were still marked all over Joshua's body.

But none of the searing pain those bruises brought could compare to the utter devastation it felt to have a father that couldn't love his son. But here he was...hearing a man who had grown to embody Joshua's most terrifying nightmares testify to his utter joy of finally having a child. Joshua wanted to scream in agony. He wanted to smash his hands against the bark of a nearby tree.

But he composed himself, recognizing that he couldn't afford to be captured at this moment.

However, he now faced a tantalizing conundrum. He could either continue reading his Father's diary in the hopes of uncovering whatever bitter secrets lie in the depths of his enigmatic origins and suffer the cost of truth. Or he could remain ignorant, throw the book away and venture off into whatever wild journey that awaited him. One thing was certain however, Joshua was a boy without a mother.

Born a Crime

Charles P. Hudson approached the front of Clairemont Hospital. It was a rather chilly midnight, and there he stood rooted to the ground, full of hesitation. Killing grandmothers wasn't particularly a hobby of old man Charles, but it was what the boss ordered, and more importantly, it was crucial to what lay ahead for the town of Clairemont. Unbeknownst to his boss, he had plans of his own up his sleeve, and killing Joshua's grandmother was a part of the puzzle.

Taking a moment to clean his large spectacles with a cloth and slowly putting them back on, Charles entered the hospital through the clear glass doors. Everyone at the front desk froze where they were the moment he entered. Charles' reputation as one of Wallace's most loyal henchmen had clearly preceded him. Charles gazed at the woman at the front desk with his stern eyes, devoid of charm. "I'm looking for a Mrs. Marilyn McCarthy." The lady shook for a moment, searching for words. "Floor-Floor number four sir," she stammered in a fit of anxiety.

Charles nodded and headed up the elevator. This couldn't be similar to other assassination attempts Charles had executed. The boss demanded subtlety so it couldn't be demonstrably traced back to him. A clear-cut assassination would merely shatter to pieces Wallace's already fragile reputation amongst the townspeople. He required the grandmother killed to bait the child into returning to Clairemont without "fomenting rebellion" as Mr. Wallace had put it.

Upon arriving at the fourth floor Charles searched for Claudia, the hospital's top doctor. Upon reaching her, he briskly hit her from the backside. Claudia looked at Charles with a frown, but he replied with a subtle grin "Can we talk in your office for a moment ma'am?"

***

Claudia shook her head. "I can't do this Charles. It's downright fucked up. I will not murder a patient of mine." Rejecting the answer, Charles slammed his hand on the desk in front of him. "You know I can't accept that answer Claudia! The boss needs that bitch dead and if you won't do it voluntarily, he'll make me force your hand." Claudia bit her tongue with such vigor that it began to sting. It may have sounded cliche, but she chose her profession to help people and had an oath to look after her patients to the best of her ability. But when billionaire tycoon Robert Wallace asks for his will to be executed, he would undoubtedly be unencumbered by any obstacles.

Claudia instantly wiped the tears that began to crawl down her face. "I'll do it Charles. Fuck it. I'll do it. But I hope you realize the two of us are gonna be burning in hell for eternity." Charles gave a light snicker. "I've been through worse than hell ma'am. That's what drives my every action." Claudia gazed into Charles' eyes for a moment, puzzled. "These pills right here should do the trick missy." Gently dropping a bottle of pills on the table, he exited the room in a carefree fashion, as if he had just handed her innocuous medicine and not a murder weapon. Resigned to the position of accepting her inevitable task, Claudia gave a heavy sigh. The pills she was provided with were exceptionally toxic. The moment the old lady would take them, she was bound to drop dead.

In no hurry, Claudia took the pills and began to fill up the glass of water. Completing the task in a sedated fashion, she began to approach Mrs. McCarthy with the water and medicine. Claudia utilized her full capacity to restrain from bursting in tears. Her father was a stoic man, and taught her about emotional restraint, which certainly came in handy as she approached the patient. As she approached, Mrs. McCarthy's eyes began to gaze upon her. They were glowing with her usual optimistic fervor. Claudia stood steadfast for a moment. It wasn't too late. She could throw the medications away and face whatever was thrown her way. She could redeem her soul and avoid eternal torment. But she had a daughter...she couldn't leave her motherless. Or worse, what if they targeted her daughter?

Claudia gulped and forced a smile. Mrs. McCarthy's face was glowing as always. "Heyyyyyyyy Madeline! Are you enjoying your night so far?" A noise emitted from the old woman indicating satisfaction. "Goooood. Very good.

Anyways sweetie, we've been closely monitoring your health and our medical research team has finally found a drug that can significantly speed up your recovery!" Claudia didn't even observe how Madeline had reacted. Everything was beginning to feel like a blur as the gravity of the situation crept into every facet of Claudia's conscience, leaving her internally paralyzed. Claudia placed the medicine and water next to the patient and sprinted out of the room. She ran into the women's restroom and began pummeling the mirror with her fist. Her hands bled but the searing pain wouldn't register in her brain, simmering with revulsion. She burst out in tears, her feet collapsing to the floor. "What have I done? WHAT THE FUCK IS WRONG WITH ME?" Claudia speedily began reciting verses from the gospel, shaking and brimming with tears. A few feet away, Madeline began prying open the bottle of pills...

***

Joshua gazed up at the magnificent moonlight, searing into his soul. His father's journal stood in his grasp. Inside himself, a war was raging between fear and curiosity. But ultimately Joshua chose curiosity and opened his father's diary, prepared to complete the story he began. The chilly breeze slapped past Joshua's sullen face as he began observing the pages once again with his utmost attention. Flipping through the pages, he was struck by his father's solemn words of satisfaction. The pages were brimming with hope. Hope for the prospects of finally starting a family with the man he loved. They expressed his father's tenacity, overcoming the burden of secrecy by sharing it with his lover. The man Joshua witnessed as he digested page by page of this magnificent journal was a man who was directly antithetical to who Joshua knew, further exacerbating Joshua's confusion and desire to discover his father's breaking point. But Joshua would soon discover that some secrets are better left unheard as he finally reached the most harrowing and tumultuous pages within the journal...

February 24, Dear Diary,
Steven is currently at Clairemont Hospital. He fainted recently from stress because of all the excessive pressure he's recently dealt with. It can't be easy to anxiously seclude yourself from society to escape the inevitable stigmatization of carrying a baby as a man. The hospital promised it wouldn't leak any information about Steven, but my gut tells me they lied. I could swear I walked past several people whose eyes flickered towards me with very peculiar looks. I paid little attention to my surroundings, however, and went to the Flower shop to buy a plant that was very special to Steven, the Myosotis Sylvatica.

He had sent me trudging through the forest one rainy day, just to share these mystical blue flowers to me. Steven spoke little when I went to the hospital today and handed him the flowers. I asked to make sure the hospital was treating him well, but his reply was an unconvincing nod, leaving me struck with a bit of anxiety. Surely these professionals would properly care for Steven? I was probably working myself up over nothing!

Joshua gazed at the page for a moment, his eyes were very wet, but that wasn't entirely a consequence of the grief that had struck him like lightning in this most sorrowful of nights. His eyes were also wet from the sweet beauty that life possessed in a subtle way, something the journal he held was brimming with, something he seldom felt when he wasn't with his grandmother. He gazed at the Myosotis Sylvatica in front of him and could finally grasp why it struck his conscience with such fervor when he first laid eyes upon it. The plant was not merely a paragon of beauty, but a representation of the love Joshua's fathers felt for each other.

Joshua continued to entrench himself into the journals pages as he gently wiped his eyes. But the subtle beauties of life would begin to dissipate before Joshua's mind as he further investigated the Journal's contents. Joshua reached a page in the diary that began to emanate with a unique aura, a tense sensation pulsating within him. The words were smeared with tears, and the writing substantially lost its articulative and legible quality, almost as though it was written by another man...

February 29, Dear Diary,
I haven't written here for days. I just couldn't, the stress of seeing Steven dealing with childbirth was too much to bear. IT'S THEIR FAULT. I'M TELLING YOU. THESE "DOCTORS". THEY ARE THE REASON HIS GONE. I cannot anymore. I'm done. I have no reason to keep living other than to sulk in misery. These fucking "doctors". They let him die because he was a gay trans man. They let him die. I saw it with my own fucking eyes.

They spent more time tending to the needs of a boy with a small bruise than they did a pregnant man giving fucking birth! This is murder. I can't live without him. I can't. This town, these people, they are evil. They must pay. They must pay. They showed me the baby boy. My baby boy. He survived the birthing process. I should've been happy. I should've been gleaming with joy. But when I looked into the little baby's eyes, I felt anger. I felt resentment. I gave him some corny ass name, Joshua, or

something. I don't give a fuck. I need steven. I need Steven now. I'm only writing this journal entry because it's my last plea for help. My life is no more. There is no difference between God or Satan. It's all the same shit. This town is a curse. This boy is a curse. This boy has killed my love.

The diary slipped from Joshua's fingers and fell to the forest grounds. He understood now. He understood everything. Joshua could vividly recall the day his Bible studies teacher told him everyone was born of sin. It was their very essence, for Adam gave into temptation at the Garden of Eden. Joshua always found himself snickering at these silly stories. But Joshua was truly born of sin. He was born as a plague. He killed his own father and left his other father to rot in misery. All because he was born. Every single relentlessly cruel insult thrown at him by the community was justified. Everyone was correct. He was a degenerate. A freak. Absolute scum on this Earth. Joshua was prepared now to turn himself over. Face the unpleasant music that awaited him. But first he had to visit someone, one last time.

Family Affairs

Joshua had to be very subtle as he sought to reconcile with his father one last time, before his inevitable acclimation towards the fiery pits of hell. His home was very deep into the depths of the town, and Robert Wallace along with his puppet mayor, clearly had spies and heavy surveillance mechanisms throughout the area to try and capture him. Joshua could hear loud noises from a distance, it must've been the sounds of an angry mob searching for him. What else could it be? Joshua quickly picked up an unconvincing disguise at a nearby shop, consisting of a fake mustache, and a gray wig. It was a ridiculous outfit, and it certainly garnered a couple stares, but he was clear of trouble or too much suspicion. When Joshua finally entered the front yard of his small one-story home, he found himself shaking, his body imbued with a sense of existential dread seldom experienced by man. He had no idea how things would unfold but he needed a sense of closure. He needed to assuage his guilt, see his father, the man he never truly understood till now, one final time. Joshua walked up to the front door; its surface was full of all sorts of cracks that would leave anyone puzzled as to how they could've managed to get there in the first place. It was in disrepair, like the entirety of the house. Joshua knocked on the door twice, gulping as he did so. Nobody responded, as expected. His father almost never allowed anyone entry into the house, regardless of context or circumstances. Joshua gave a heavy sign and kicked the door wide open, snapping the hinges as he did so. He heard his father's raspy voice give an indifferent response, "what the fuck do you want." Not the reply you'd typically expect from a homeowner who gets their door kicked open.

"Listen dad, I just wanted to talk to you about something." His father replied with an audible snicker. "Talk? What do you want to talk about, son? Wanna discuss our favorite movie trilogies? What video games do we wanna play next?" His father was masterful at the art of sarcasm, it was quite remarkable. "I know why you hate me dad. And I'm really really sorry. I just wish you told me." His father stood up from his recliner and gazed absentmindedly at Joshua.

He ruffled his mustache for a minute and replied. "Yea I hate you cuz you're a punk. A low life. A travesty to all of humanity. You make Hitler look like a choir boy, son." Joshua removed his store-bought wig and facial hair and shook his head.

"I know about Steven, father." With those five words, the

room went quiet. An aura of uncertainty pervaded Joshua's mind but he was hopeful that his father would open up. That the years of malice shared between the two would finally evaporate. But that thought proved itself to be a pipedream moment later as his father lunged at Joshua with a scream that was likely audible from miles away. He grabbed his neck tight and began to scream into Joshua's face, the spit indiscriminately spraying him in the process. **"DON'T YOU EVER UTTER THAT MAN'S NAME YOU SCUMBAG. YOU KILLED HIM. YOU ARE THE REASON I SUFFER EVERY MOMENT OF MY LIFE, WITHOUT A MOMENT TO ESCAPE THE ABYSS OF MY UTTER MISERY."** Joshua burst into tears, unable to contain the guilt within him that was eating at his soul. His father's verbal provocation transformed into an intense physical assault as he began to pummel his fist against Joshua's face, making an indecipherable noise with his mouth as he did so. His face was bloodied beyond belief as it continued to be pummeled by his father, but Joshua felt no internal desire to resist. In fact, in a crude way, Justice was being served for what he had done.

With a few more blows, it was clear Joshua would be gone, lost forever in the endless cycle of life and death, but before the fatal blow manifested, in less than a second, a loud bang emitted from outside and without a moment's notice, his father fell to the floor with a thud. At that moment Joshua should've been left puzzled, but he was too damaged, inside and out, to reflect upon the unfolding events. He stood where he was, content with the prospect of bleeding to death. He deserved it anyways. Slowly, Joshua began drifting away…

***

Joshua opened his eyes, his eye lids searing with pain as he did so. He touched his face, feeling bandages on virtually every inch of it. He wasn't dead. Somebody must've stopped the bleeding. Likely the same person who killed his father. "Hello there young man!" Joshua shot up from the couch he was lying on. He knew that voice, very clearly in fact. He was in some sort of apartment, surrounded by a plethora of different exotic paintings from various historical eras, covering most of the walls. "Mr. Hudson?" Suddenly a man appeared from behind him, Joshua's European history teacher. He seemed far more physically apt and impressive, a sense of confidence exuding from him that wasn't present when he taught history.

Joshua should've been brimming with questions. Questions that were so brazenly obvious such as why he was in his European history teachers' room with bandages on. And whether this old geezer was the man who shot down his father and saved his life. Unfortunately, Joshua didn't even care one iota. "Look sir, I appreciate these gestures but you should've let me die.

You shouldn't have shot down my father. I'm the villain in this story." The old man firmly shook his head. "Look, kid I don't know what you did to your father or how badly you fucked up, but pummeling someone's face till they slowly bleed to death isn't justice. That's even cruel for my standards." Joshua wasn't sure what that last bit meant but he rolled his eyes and laid back down on his couch.

"I just want this fucking nightmare to end. I don't want to stay any longer on this planet." The old man's response to his comments shocked Joshua. "You fucking pussy." Joshua shot back up from his couch. "Excuse me sir?" "Oh, you heard me, boy. You're a goddamn pussy!" Joshua was bewildered beyond imagination. "Pussy? Pussy? Do you even know what I did to get here? I literally saved a little kid from getting his ass beat, I basically signed my fucking death warrant in the process. Don't call me a pussy, sir." "And yet here you are moping away in misery as the man who killed your grandmother is out there trying to put a bullet in your head and end your family lineage for good!" For once, Joshua's confusion was lit with a frightened curiosity. "What? What are you talking about?"

Mr. Hudson seemed to light up, as if he was giddily waiting to report this information to Joshua. He pulled a newspaper from underneath the table and shoved it in front of Joshua's face. The Headline made Joshua's heart sink, **"eighty-four-Year-Old Woman Found Dead Due to Medical Complications."** Joshua didn't have the patience or will to skim through the article. He placed the paper on the table and stood, in silence. It was not clear how much time had passed, the room was pitch quiet, Mr. Hudson, sensitive enough to recognize that speaking now would only make matters worse.

***

Clairemont mayor Douglas Harrison gazed outside the windows of Town Hall to the sight of absolute pandemonium. Clairemont was typically a docile town with little resistance. In fact, protests were regarded as "liberal hippy" behavior unbecoming of a Christian polity. But somehow the death of an old hag had triggered an unprecedented response amongst the public. Absolutely nobody bought the official town report that she had died of a medical complication. Stones, tomatoes and various assortments of objects were being thrown at the government building and the people, in the hundreds, were actively resisting the town police deployed to disperse the crowds. Douglas had never signed up for this utter nonsense. He had accepted donations from Robert Wallace because he was promised political victory but now his life was on the line. These people were ready to bash skulls, ready to finally overthrow the status quo that marginalized them to a state of fear for so long. Shaking with pure anxiety, Douglas picked up his phone and typed the numbers to call his financier, the infamous Robert Wallace.

"Robert. Absolutely nobody is buying your story. They think you're responsible for killing that old bitch. And they're pissed at me. Don't make me regret taking your money Robert. Fix this right fucking now." Douglas hung up the phone before Robert could reply. Gritting his teeth together, Douglas held back his tears. The chants from the mob became louder and louder as the day progressed.

Hang Robert Wallace
The Devil in Sheep's Clothing the Butcher of Clairemont
Hang Robert Wallace
Several miles from town hall, Charles Hudson sat relaxed on his couch, a sinister smile emanating from his face as he watched the protesters rock the town of Clairemont from his television. A few feet away, Joshua was lying on the bed Mr. Hudson had lent him. He was so exhausted from crying; he could shed only a few tears for his dear grandmother. But he was experiencing a sense of clarity and purpose that had escaped his grasp for the last few days. He would avenge his grandmother. He was going to kill Robert Wallace.

Joshua slowly crawled out of bed and took a seat next to Mr. Hudson. "Let's get rid of this mother fucker."

PART II
The Lost Sister

Forty-five Years Ago...
Charles gazed into his sister's light blue eyes. "Are you sure you're gonna be okay Gazebella? Give me a call the second you need my attention. I'm always here for you." Gazebella giggled. "I'll be fine silly, it's just a high school party!" Charles smiled. "Well all right, I hope you have a blast!" Gazebella nodded and left the car to head towards her friend Dominic's house. This was the first high school party she had ever been to, the thought of which made her simultaneously nervous and brimming with excitement.

As she entered the house, a sense of utter alienation began to permeate throughout every inch of her body. Gazebella was a quiet book worm and an absolute nerd. Her idea of a good time was being snuggled up in bed reading the Hobbit or playing the latest Wii game with her online friends. But this party atmosphere was a whole 'nother beast. Bright lights were flashing through every inch of the home, leaving Gazebella utterly disoriented. There were screams and chatter emitting throughout the home, not a hint of solitude present in the building. Gazebella scurried throughout the house looking for Dominic. Nobody here seemed remotely familiar, it was almost as though she was transported into a whole 'nother dimension with fundamentally distinct norms, values and properties.

After searching for a few more minutes, Gazebella decided it was a lost cause and decided to sit down on a couch. She could feel the presence of several men awkwardly gazing at her or in some cases flickering their eyes towards her direction and quickly turning back to avoid getting caught. Gazebella rolled her eyes. "Creeps," she whispered to herself. The first instinct Gazebella had was to contact her brother and get the fuck out of this mad house. But she had just arrived, and she didn't want to disturb him, especially considering how busy he was with his college preparations.

Gazebella ultimately decided to head towards the mini bar at the corner of the house. She had never consumed a drop of alcohol in her life before and was hoping there would be non-alcoholic beverages. Unfortunately, there didn't seem to be any chocolate milk or lemonade present. Gazebella stared at the lineup of beverages. The school pastor told all the students that consuming even a drop of non-pure alcoholic beverages was an act of treason against God. But Gazebella had to grow up eventually. And besides, how else would she pass her time in this nightmare?

"One drop." She assured herself. Gazebella picked up the bottle of vodka and a glass, pouring herself a tiny amount of the drink. After consuming just a modest amount, she instantly spit the drink out of her mouth in absolute revulsion. "You okay Gazebella?" Gazebella turned to her right and there Dominic stood, trying his utmost to hold back a laugh. Gazebella tried to repress her flustered state of mind and reacted by rolling her eyes. "Oh, shut up dude."

"Hey Gazebella? You wanna go somewhere quiet?" It was as if Dominic could read her state of mind. If it was any other guy the thought of going someplace quiet during the middle of a party would be a frightening proposition, but there was a lovable and trustworthy quality to Dominic. A feeling of intimate warmth behind his self-assured smile, a feeling that Gazebella rarely experienced with men.

The two headed towards an empty bedroom, and awkwardly sat down next to one another. The tension in the room was palpable and less than a split second later, they began making out. Gazebella had never even touched another boy's lips in her life, let alone engaged in an intense make out session, and hoped to god she wasn't doing anything incorrectly. Dominic began to go on top of Gazebella, kissing her slender neck, and was beginning the motion of pulling down her black skirt when Gazebella interjected. "Dominic! Stop! We aren't supposed to have sex Dominic. It's against the very principles Christ gave his life up for."

Dominic stopped what he was doing for a moment and stared into Gazebella. But his gaze wasn't radiating with the same warm and vibrant energy it typically exuded. Instead, it was a look of bewilderment and embarrassment. A few moments later, Dominic stood up and nodded. "You're right Gazebella. That was inappropriate. I'm very sorry." He solemnly exited the room, leaving Gazebella to contemplate upon the peculiar series of events that had just gone down. Gazebella gazed into her sweaty palms for a moment and shook her head. She picked up her phone to call her big brother. Who knew parties could be so damn stressful?

***

Charles wasn't able to go to sleep that night. Something about his sister just felt off. She had assured him the party went fine but her facial expressions told a vastly different story. She appeared petrified. Charles had an unhealthy attachment to his sister. His schoolmates would tease him and suggest it was an "incestuous relationship," but it was far more profound and wasn't sexual in its nature. It was his responsibility to care for his sister because he was the only true parent she had. Their mother had passed away years ago in her battle with heroin addiction and their father was a drunk, out of control maniac who somehow qualified to be a police officer for the town of Clairemont. Just went to show that personal responsibility wasn't relevant to attain power if you were a man.

Their father was a faithful man, but he used faith to justify beating and abusing Charles and his sister for minor infractions. His justifications always arose from the ten commandments. "You must respect your parents," he would assert. As if accidently buying the wrong bottle of booze for your father was a major act of disrespect. Charles was the only shoulder for Gazebella to cry on every time her father went on his typical verbal tirades and physical punishments. One day her father told Gazebella he regretted "she was ever born on this planet and would've aborted her if he was a damn liberal." Charles spent hours trying to reassure Gazebella how important and valuable she was to him and to God that day.

But this time around it was going to be vastly more difficult. Because his sister was in immense pain. And Charles had absolutely no clue why. A room away Gazebella rested her face on a pillow, screaming and crying into it with utter despair. But she couldn't fully grasp where that despair derived from. She was attracted to Dominic. She desperately wanted to gain his approval. But why did she have to act like such a bitch? Why couldn't she just enjoy herself for once and not let faith get in her way? But if she let him penetrate her, she would also be full of guilt right now. It was as though she would cry no matter how she reacted to the circumstances. "At least the hurt feelings would disappear tomorrow," she thought to herself.

It was the first period in Clairemont High the next day, and Gazebella stared at her algebra test, incapable of maintaining her focus for even a second. She had felt a sense of absolute detachment from her surroundings, in fact from her very own body the moment she walked into the school building. She was likely going to get a zero on this godforsaken exam but at the moment she simply didn't care. Suddenly, an announcement was made on the school speaker. "Attention all students of Clairemont High. We have an urgent meeting. All students gather in the auditorium." Gazebella froze for a moment but shrugged a few seconds later and internally laughed at herself. Of course, this meeting wasn't going to be about her. She hadn't even done anything wrong!

The hundreds of students of Clairemont High, from Freshman to Seniors, took a seat at the school auditorium. The school's head pastor, Richard Grenell, stood in front of a podium on the stage. His face was lit up with pure anguish and he held a wooden cross firmly in his hands. The audience was quieted by his very presence. The man began to speak, his cranky, yet booming voice permeating throughout the room.

"Students of Clairemont High. I have no desire to prolong this conversation and therefore will begin right away. It has come to my attention that a freshman student at this high school has engaged in an unholy act of deviancy, and utter degeneracy. I was informed today that a vile act of premarital sex was initiated by a girl in this high school." The auditorium was now filled with the sound of boos and expressions of dismay. Gazebella began slowly sweating. The pastor continued, "As you are all aware, the act of sex exists for the sole purpose of multiplying the human species. It is only appropriate to engage in such an act after you have been blessed in the holy union between man and woman. The bible teaches us that."

Before the pastor could continue his lecture, Gazebella shot up from her seat. "I did not have sex with a man sir. Whoever told you this is lying! I understand that God doesn't allow us to have sex till marriage!" Suddenly, the auditorium began to be filled with murmurs and light snickers. A wicked grin began to emanate from the pastor's face. "Since when did I utter your name misses?" Gazebellas heart began to sink. It was a trap. This was the goddamn punishment. Public humiliation. Now every single person in this town would think Gazebella was a degenerate, satanic rebel of God. She could feel her brother's gaze from across the auditorium where the seniors sat, but she couldn't work up the courage to look into his eyes.

Gazebella sunk into her seat, tears gently dropping from her eyes. "Dominic, you lying son of a bitch," she whispered to herself.

Gazebella darted back home the moment the assembly ended. She could hear moaning noises and people calling her a slut as she ran. She locked the door to her room and jumped onto bed, exploding with tears. Everyone thought she was a freak. She was being castigated by the city of Clairemont for something she had never even done! There was a sudden knock on Gazebella's door. It had to be her brother. She worked up her courage and opened the door.

Charles rushed up to Gazebella and gave her the tightest hug imaginable. She could feel his tears and sorrow as they tightly embraced one another. "I'm so fucking sorry Gazebella. I'm so sorry." The two of them spent the night together, in a tight embrace, crying their souls out. Charles kissed her forehead. "It'll be okay Gazebella. It'll be okay. I promise you." Gazebella was quiet. She couldn't tell her brother the sinister thoughts that began to encroach her mind, or he would certainly intervene.

The next morning Gazebella walked into Clairemont High, unfazed by her surroundings. She knew that virtually everyone she walked across was observing her. She could see the facial expressions people made mocking her. When she approached her locker, she witnessed the word SLUT written in red with paint. But none of it really mattered. Gazebella left school as the bell rang and patiently waited for the pitch-black night to approach. When she was certain her father and Charles were asleep, she snuck into her father's drawer and grabbed his firearm.

Thirty-five Years Later: Present Time

Joshua and Charles sat on the couch together and watched the local news. Joshua wasn't typically interested in current events but the town of Clairemont was witnessing unrest like never before seen in the town's history, small businesses being looted, buildings on fire, the clashes between police and residents had only exacerbated in their severity as time passed. Joshua noticed that his history teacher, Charles Hudson, was particularly enthralled by the series of events. Out of curiosity, Joshua decided to further enquire. "Hey Mr. Hudson. I truly appreciate all that you've done to help me and I'm grateful that you'll help me secure my vengeance. But why do you care so much? What did Wallace do to you?" Charles gazed into the TV screen, transfixed by the images flickering on the screen. "Look at these animals. The whole lot of them. It's not just Robert Wallace, my boy. I think it's about time Nero played his tune anew."

On the Brink

Charles Hudson solemnly gazed into the tombstone of his dearly departed sister Gazebella. He visited Clairemont cemetery every day to spend time with her, ever since her departure. It helped add a sense of clarity to his mission and bolstered his sense of resolve. Charles reached down and gently kissed the tombstone. "I will make this city pay Gazebella. I will make it pay for what it did to you. I am giving birth to a powerful weapon. He will plunge civilization into the fiery pits of hell." Charles rested his face against the tombstone, gently weeping. Meanwhile, a relatively significant distance away, Joshua visited a local diner he had never once laid foot on. There was nothing particularly unique about the establishment. It featured a light pink exterior; the paint job was clearly half assed. Inside there were a few tables and seats scattered around the small interior.

However, despite its seemingly insignificant quality, this was the diner where Joshua's fathers met each other. The waiter visited Joshua as he took a seat at a table. Joshua simply flickered a smile his way but ordered nothing. The image of his father first meeting Steven at the diner flickered before his mind as he gazed out the window. Joshua felt a sense of security here, as if his other father was gazing at him from the heavens. The waiter approached Joshua once again. "Sir, if you're not gonna order something, we're gonna have to ask you to leave." Hearing those words, Joshua froze. "Sir." Joshua was used to being called sir. It was so prevalent wherever he visited, and he never put much thought into it. After all he was a male right? A peculiar male, but a male, nonetheless. But when the waiter said it this time, a jarring sensation emitted within Joshua. As if something felt wrong.

For a moment Joshua entered a phase of absolute derealization, as if his entire existence was merely a mythology constructed by his psyche. But as the waiter continued to hassle Joshua, he was plunged back to reality.

"Right. Umm. I'll have some green tea. Thank you." The waiter curtly nodded and left. Joshua dropped his face onto the table, a painful sensation searing into his insides. He wasn't a female, he couldn't be. He had to be strong, assertive, and repress his deviant thoughts. It's the only way he could get his revenge. Joshua's disguise was beginning to make him itch in discomfort, and with that, he jumped up from his table and headed out the door.

***

Robert Wallace rummaged through his wardrobe to find his absolute best suit and dress pants. Swiftly and half mindedly, he put on his clothes and looked at the mirror in disgust. Pitch black eyes, a double chin, and an overall chubby body structure looked back at him. "How could a man of my stature, my brilliance, my ingenuity fuck up this badly?" Robert thought to himself. The town of Clairemont was suffering through absolute chaos, local government officials were resigning in unprecedented numbers, and major companies were beginning to pull their investments from the town. And just as it seemed like things couldn't possibly get worse, the mayor of the urban center of Chataluma now called Mr. Wallace up for a meeting. Robert spent inordinate amounts of time trying to find clever ways to ignore the Clairemont mayor, but he simply couldn't do the same for the powerful and newly elected Mayor Joseph Hellenburger of Chataluma. Robert gave a loud sigh and got in his vehicle. "Let's hope this trip isn't an unmitigated disaster," he whispered to himself.

forty minutes later, Robert Wallace sat in front of the great mayor. He was even more overweight than Robert was, had a face that resembled a walrus, and a giant white beard that simply wasn't compatible with his other features. The mayor gazed at Robert with a stern face. "Mr. Wallace!

You have been a good, trustworthy friend to me for a long time. Some of my best memories come from our early years fucking over grandmothers with our over expensive health insurance plans." The mayor snickered. "But now, I'm at the peak of my career! Newly elected mayor of this goddamn district for Christ's sake, and you fuck me over!" The walrus-like man slammed his hand on the Mayoral desk. Robert continued to listen attentively, stiff and silent. "forty billion goddamn dollars. That's how much money they invested into my campaign Robert. All the wealthy industrialists, all the great pharma and health insurance CEOs. They ran advertisements up the wazoo for my fucking campaign because I made a promise."

"I made a promise that I would revitalize this goddamn economy. Privatize everything. Bring jobs, create a safe, stable, and prosperous tax haven for my patriotic financiers." The mayor nodded with furious passion, brimming with intensity. "But then you had to kill a fucking grandmother. A GRANDMOTHER FOR CHRISTS SAKE ROBERT. WHAT THE FUCK IS WRONG WITH YOU?" Robert stood up from his seat. "It was a medical error sir!" The mayor snorted out with laughter. "You mistake me for somebody who gives a shit Robert. The people, in the thousands, are ransacking Clairemont. It's a goddamn mad house over there. My investors are shitting their pants, gritting their teeth. They're scared, that mess is gonna come to Chataluma." "Sir, I have taken aggressive measures to counter this misinformation and the mayor has directed the town's active-duty forces to shut down this chaos."

"Well, clearly it isn't enough! Don't you understand Robert? These protesters represent the death kneel of our civilized capitalist order. They will inspire others. People will be thinking in their heads now, if these loyal Christian loonies can stand up to the wealthy, to our civilized order, why can't we? I don't care what you do Robert. Hire private militias. Rattle your pussy mayor into declaring martial law and shoot as many unpatriotic degenerates as you so desire. Just fix this mess or all our heads are gonna be on a platter. Do I make myself clear?" Robert nodded. "Yes sir."

***

Joshua and Mr. Hudson silently ate their dinner together in Mr. Hudson's apartment, Josuha's last and only refuge. "You enjoying the salad kid? My sister taught me the recipe. She had all kinds of delicious vegan combinations." Joseph nodded. "It's good sir." Charles gazed at Joshua through his spectacles as he gobbled down his meal. "Is something bothering you kid?" Joshua's serene eyes looked up and gazed into Charles. "Sir, did you ever feel like you weren't a man? Like you didn't belong in your body?" Joshua didn't expect much from asking his former history teacher the question, but he was desperately curious, attempting to grasp at whatever could help resolve his identity crisis.

To his immense surprise, Mr. Hudson smiled and solemnly looked at Joshua. "Why kid? You having some troubles?" Joshua reflexively became defensive. "No sir! Not at all. I'm just curious, that's all." "Well, I'm gonna say something very peculiar, I hope you don't judge me too hard kid."

Joshua shook his head with a smile. "Trust me sir, I can't judge jackshit. I'm as close to an anti-Christ as they come."

"Well, I always felt uncomfortable with myself. I didn't feel much animosity towards my body, in fact I cherished and continue to cherish it heavily. But I never really saw myself as a man. The weird thing is, I never saw myself as a woman neither. I loved wearing cool shirts and all the trendy male fashion of my time. I loved playing violent video games and getting physical. But I also had a feminine side. I never told my friends my fascination with knitting. My endearment for romantic comedies. My love for dresses that I was too pussy to try on. I don't know, kid. I wish there was some third category ya know? Not male, not female. That'd probably be me." Charles chuckled. "Insane am I right?" "No sir, that's the most sane thing I've ever heard."

Joshua looked down at his unfinished salad, the tomatoes, lettuce, and dressing were all over the place, because he was absentmindedly playing with his food. "Charles was clearly insane," Joshua thought to himself. But so was he. They were basically two peas in a pod.

A Moral Dilemma

Charles Hudson absentmindedly sat through the night, an intense sensation of guilt pulsating within himself. He had killed this boy's grandmother. Of course, if it wasn't him, another one of Wallace's henchmen would've struck her down. But her blood was on his hands. An innocent woman, Joshua's last sliver of connection. Most grotesque of all, Charles was increasingly becoming a father figure to Joshua. He killed Joshua's last remaining family and was slowly beginning to take their place.

Beethoven's Ode to Joy permeated throughout Charles' bedroom as he sat, semidetached from his surroundings. The most infuriating thing to Charles was the fact that he would've done it again. He would've killed that grandmother in cold blood, setting the grounds to finally get revenge on this town for killing his fucking innocent sister. Speaking to Joshua, feeling his solemn, tortured presence, shined a light upon Charles dead and cruel heart, but the desire for vengeance still tickled stronger.

Charles' phone began ringing, piercing through Beethoven's masterpiece. It was Robert Wallace. Charles picked it up and answered, bereft of all passion. "Hey, what do you want?" He could hear Wallace's heavy breathing emitting from the call. The man was clearly broken and within his tipping point. "Charles. Why is the boy still alive? Do you even have an idea of where he might be? Don't forget your mission, Charles." Wallace spoke in a way that attempted to be assertive but came off as desperate and unhinged. "Mr. Wallace, relax. I promise you I will find and capture this boy. But are you sure you still want this? The town is already shaking from the unfortunate demise of the boy's grandmother." The call ended. Wallace had hung up.

Charles gave a loud snicker. Thus far, he didn't have to do anything to slowly bring about the collapse of this town. Robert Wallace, and his arrogant stupidity was doing all the work for him. He peeked out of his apartment window. It seemed as though the mayor's implementation of Martial law and heavy security had scared the town's people into submission. There were officers at every checkpoint, vigilant and ready to shoot anybody who was insubordinate. "This is the calm before the storm," Charles whispered to himself with a smile.

The next morning, after getting a mere two hours of sleep, Charles woke up, prepared for a big day. Robert Wallace was about to make a significant announcement to the town and Charles was invited as a trusted member of the town's regime. Charles briefly visited Joshua in the next-door room. He had just woken up, rubbing his eyes as he laid in bed. "Listen kid, I'm gonna be back in a few hours. Make sure to stay the fuck put and don't do anything stupid." Joshua nodded, "sounds reasonable enough."

Hundreds of people gathered in front of the town hall, awaiting the great Robert Wallace to take the podium. If he was intelligent, Robert would make this speech an apology, a pseudo attempt at reconciliation and forgiveness. For a Christina community, such a message would be effective in rendering the desired results. But Charles was rather doubtful the speech would hit such notes. Sure enough, approximately fifteen minutes late, Robert Wallace approached the crowd, loud cheers and "hoorays" making the rounds. Of course, the entire audience was elitists loyal to the billionaire tycoon, but the setup would clearly create a perception of legitimacy for those watching from their televisions'. "Hello, fellow citizens of Clairemont!" The crowd burst with cheers before Wallace could say more. The venue was protected by an immense security force surrounding the perimeter, although that was hardly necessary because there were only a few brave protesters present, holding the crucifix, and putting up signs calling the billionaire a murderer.

"Dear citizens of Clairemont, the foundational values of our town are under attack by a loud minority of satanic deviants attempting to subvert the will of this town with their blatantly false propaganda!" The crowd's cheers and applause rang louder as Robert Wallace spoke, his voice booming with confidence and conviction. "They told you that I, a faithful Christian man, killed a poor old grandmother!" The crowd booed in unison. "The medical examiners, all the evidence from the scene, the eyewitness testimony all confirmed that this woman had died due to accidental medical malpractice, but these degenerates somehow blamed me!" The boo's continued to permeate throughout the venue, albeit with slightly less energy.

"I will tell you why they blamed me. They blamed me because I am an Ubermensch! My perfection, my masculine energy, my passionate love for perfection and domination, scare these bloody scoundrels!" At this eloquent line, the cheers became louder than ever, almost to the point of damaging Charles eardrums. "But citizens of Clairemont. I am not upset. I am not bitter. I am prouder than ever. Proud of my Christian upbringing. My special relationship to Christ.

Proud that I had a family that loved and cherished and raised me with the values of Christ! For that very reason, I am officially donating one billion dollars to the Clairemont Church, to strengthen our faith in the town, and to drive away the madness and lunacy of these radical infiltrators!" As the audience performatively went haywire at the announcement, Charles, for the first time, was plunged into a state of fear and anxiety. This was a brilliant speech. This was exactly what Robert needed to say and do to get the decadent masses on his side and to marginalize his enemies.

However, Wallace's next statement instantly got Charles' brain to start churning again. "I will sign this 1-billion-dollar check at the Clairemont Church in five days! Every loyal Christian patriot will be invited!" This was it. This was how the billionaire tyrant of Clairemont would fall, and the town with him. Charles picked up his phone and called Joshua. "Listen kid, I hope you get your ass ready. Because there's boutta be some goddamn history in the making."

***

Joshua shook his head in disbelief. "We are not going to blow up a Church sir." "Listen, kid, revenge is a dirty affair and it's never spotless. If you want to take out the son of a bitch who murdered your dear grandmother in cold blood, you have gotta make sacrifices." "Mr. Hudson, I spent most of my time sulking at humanity, perceiving my own species as devoid of any compassion or love. Worth less than dirt. But if there's anything these revolts have shown me, there is good in mankind. And by killing innocent church goers, I'm no better than the scum of this Earth." Charles shook his head, but he wasn't furious. In fact, it almost seemed as though he envied Joshua's optimism. "Joshua, the rabble of this town are only breaking their decades of conformity out of fear for their own lives. They didn't care about the endless reign of misery they imposed on those they perceived to be peculiar or decadent. To the townspeople, the death of your grandmother, a poor and aged innocent soul, represented an attack on the status quo.

How many dead queers, sexually active girls, and so-called witches have to pile up for you to realize these people are the enemy?" There was silence as Joshua and Charles laid there on the couch, full of absentminded contemplation.

"This will be an easy operation my boy. I am going to have security clearance for the church event in five days. I will place an explosive in the building, located somewhere that won't be found by even the keenest of eyes. Only the worst of humanity will be in that church, and they will burn to ashes, they will be inflicted with the same pain and misery they've inflicted on others for decades and decades Joshua." Joshua stood up. "I will kill Robert Wallace and I will look him in the eye as I do it sir. I will not bomb bystanders because of some perceived grievances I have with the collective. There will be children sir. Fucking children." Joshua became more assertive as he spoke. "And sir. If you attempt to detonate a bomb in that church, I will do everything in my ability to take you down. So, you're either with me or you can put a bullet into my skull like you did to my father. It's up to you."

Charles nodded. "You have articulated your point well young sir. But I promise you this virtuous attitude of yours will not last forever. Soon, you will realize the true depths of man's callousness." Charles began churning with thoughts. His original, foolproof plan had to be discarded and replaced with something far riskier and more daring. There was no guarantee they'd complete their mission, but there was still an opportunity to plunge this town into the pure chaos and misery it deserved for what it did to his sister. As Charles sat in contemplation of his next move, Joshua interjected. "Sir, the Church bathroom. Can you place a gun there for me to pick up during the event?" Charles slowly began to grin. "Hey, that could actually work! You could pull off that assassination Michael Corleone executed in the godfather! Of course, you'd need an effective disguise to enter the church without being recognized… But how would you get out of there alive? There would be hundreds of people there to cheer on their fabulous billionaire savior and son of Christ, not to mention a massive, concentrated police presence." The apartment room emanated with pure silence once again.

"I don't plan on getting out of there alive sir. And before you begin to protest, I hope you realize that I have nothing to live for mister. I was born an abomination to humanity, I just want to die avenging the purest soul I ever knew, my dear grandmother." Charles felt his soul slowly tearing apart. He didn't know why. It's not as though this kid was his blood relative or supposed to be more than a means to an end. But he couldn't let him die. "Look, I know life seems devoid of any meaning or purpose or joy right now Joshua. But one day you may find that spark that rekindles and replenishes you. Makes you a new man. And I will try the utmost possible, to make sure you can experience that." Joshua gazed into Charles eyes, piercing into his soul like a laser. "Did you ever have a spark sir?"

Charles nodded. "I did Joshua. In Fact, I still do."

Savior

As expected, Charles was selected to be the leader of the security oversight team for the upcoming Church event. Despite being the gravest threat to Robert Wallace's powerful regime, he also demonstrated his loyalty to the billionaire tycoon more than anyone else. That was solidified when he murdered Joshua's grandmother and completed arguably the grisliest and most gruesome acts Wallace had ever demanded. As Charles and his security team entered the church for initial security preparations, he felt an invigorating and nostalgic sense of joy at the prospect of partially implementing into practice one of the most iconic moments in movie history.

Michael Corleone's assassination of Sollazzo and the police chief from the godfather. With grace and subtlety, Charles placed the small Glock behind the toilet tank in the women's bathroom. Although Charles was hesitant of such a proposal, Joshua insisted that it would be the safest location because the security officials would be far more likely to investigate the men's bathrooms, especially considering the stereotypes embedded in the community. Besides, as uncultured and insular as the town was, clearly some of them had watched the godfather, right?

Meanwhile, as preparations were being made to orchestrate the assassination of Robert Wallace, Joshua was given vigorous firearms training by Charles. It had to be a remote location distant from the authorities, and Joshua had to make thorough preparations to disguise his identity. The first day was an unmitigated failure, with the bullets spraying everywhere, and the gun slipping from Joshua's sweaty palms on numerous occasions. Charles was a very stern instructor, unafraid to get physically and verbally intense to clean up Joshua's act. He smacked Joshua's back when his posture wasn't satisfactory and screamed ruthless insults from the top of his lungs when he failed to give his undivided attention towards Charles. "Listen here you sniveling good for nothing son of a bitch. You are gonna glue your eyes and ears towards my direction or I'm gonna slap you silly till you cry for your mother."

Despite the unconventionality of his cruel tactics, the results were undoubtedly staggering. By the third day Joshua had managed to perfect his posture, properly execute the motions to fire the gun, and shoot with immense accuracy, at one point shooting the test dummy's eyes.

Joshua gave an immense grin at the prospect that this dummy would eventually be Robert Wallace. Despite his callous demeanor, Charles was growing fonder of Joshua by the day, as the intense training sessions progressed. The kid's determination to avenge his grandmother was commendable and it reminded Charles of his own desire to see Clairemont drown in a pool of blood, to decay in the most grotesque manner, the way the city callously disposed of his sister. As the day of the church gathering grew closer, Charles knew he had to preserve this boy's life. It was the least he could do after he murdered his grandmother and father.

It was almost certain Joshua would likely lose his own life in the process of taking out Wallace, but Charles had one last ditch opportunity to give the boy at least a chance at living. Stealthily entering Town Hall, Charles swiftly glanced through a list of the townspeople's addresses the mayor kept with him until he found the woman who was complicit in murdering Joshua's grandmother, Claudia. Charles sighed heavily. The plan he was on the verge of acting out was a long shot effort, but there was hope.

***

Charles entered a small neighborhood around the edges of town. It comprised an assortment of the town's more superior homes, some of which displayed an artistic sense of eccentricity with triangle windows, and peculiar zig zaggy roofs. Many of the more expensive and impressive houses were at the periphery of the town to keep a distance from the filth and greater poverty in Clairemonts center. As he drove through the neighborhood, Charles finally reached Claudia's home. It was far more modest and simplistic compared to the rest of the neighborhood but well-kept and sweetly designed, with beautiful daffodils populating the front yard. Charles gave three loud knocks on the dark red front door. In a few moments, the door swung open and there stood Claudia. She was an absolute wreck ever since she assisted Charles in murdering the old grandmother. Her blonde hair was everywhere, her blue eyes appeared lazy and tiresome, and her eyelids restlessly opened and closed at a rapid speed.

She was wearing rags that appeared to be unwashed in possibly months.

Charles looked at her pitifully as she opened the door. He knew he was partially complicit in her current predicament and his insides couldn't help but permeate with a slight feeling of guilt. "What the fuck do you want with me Charles? I did what you asked of me. It's been slowly tearing at my soul day after day, but I did it. Are you here to murder me? My kids are fast asleep in bed, will you have them wake up motherless Charles?" With a heartfelt and genuine gaze at Claudia, Charles profusely shook his head. "Nothing like that Claudia. Nothing like that. May I enter?" Claudia opened the door wider, signaling for Charles to come in.

The two took a seat on the living room couch, there were ornaments of crosses scattered throughout the walls. The entire home was so silent for a moment that one could hear the children's snores from upstairs. Slightly ashamed of what he was about to say, Charles decided to break the silence. "Claudia, I know you are a deeply faithful woman, and I know you feel intense regret for what you did. But what if I told you there was a path towards redemption?" Claudia snickered, "And why the fuck do you care if I'm redeemed or not?" He responded with a shrug. "I normally wouldn't care that much but in these circumstances your redemption would be in my best interests, although I won't disclose why." Claudia stood up from the couch and gave what appeared to be a tormented grin. "You've come back to fuck me over again, haven't you? Get out. Get the fuck out of my house and NEVER COME BACK CHARLES."

Charles replied by gently placing his pointer finger

against his lips, indicating to Claudia that she should quiet down. "The kids will wake up if you don't quiet down ma'am," he gently whispered. Gazing at Charles with a dismayed expression, she sat back down. "Please, before you cast judgment, listen to me Claudia. Ultimately, this will be your choice." Claudia sat where she was, utterly frozen. "I can sense ma'am that you're a very devout woman. A believer in Christ and the gospels. My cynicism unfortunately precludes me from having such a wholesome relationship with the divine, but I appreciate your attachment to divinity." Charles paused for a moment, allowing his words to sink in. "I recognize Claudia that I directed you towards a sinful act, I coerced you into murdering an innocent soul. Worse, I coerced you into spitting all over your lord and savior."

Charles grabbed a lighter from his pocket and swiftly flickered it on and off. "Have you ever burned yourself in an accident? Perhaps even on purpose Claudia?" Charles noticed that Claudia's frozen demeanor began shaking slightly. "I've been burnt before. Numerous times actually. It's quite the painful experience, leaving you searing with pain for up to days on end." Charles slowly shook his head, a subtly daunting look appearing on his face. "Now imagine your entire body covered in the most unpleasant of flames. Your breasts, fingers, legs, stomach, all encompassed by the pure horror of hell's pit." Charles insincerely gulped, to emphasize the horrors of what he described.

"Claudia, you can repent all you want. But for the horrors of what you inflicted on that poor old woman; this may be your eternal fate. That is, unless you take part in an equally benevolent act to counter it." Once again, there was a moment of bleak silence. Charles noticed that Claudia's eyes were beginning to tear up, until she completely burst out crying. It was a cry so intense, so terrifying, that Charles began to drown in a fiery sense of guilt he had seldom experienced.

Claudia tried to construct a sentence in between the tears and screams of absolute terror. "What-What do you want me to do Charles?"

"I need you to go to a paper and confess, Claudia. Fuck it, you can tell them that I instructed you to kill that grandmother. But tell them you killed that old lady, and that Robert Wallace was the one who orchestrated this atrocity." Claudia shook her head, but without the same assertiveness as she had prior. "Charles. I have children I must raise and care for. If I do what you ask of me," Charles cut her off, "What the lord asks of you Claudia." "If I do this Charles, I'll either be in prison for a long time or murdered. My children will be doomed to suffer." Charles stood up from where he sat. "Perhaps. But do you really believe your children will be better off raised by a guilt-stricken woman who clearly can't get her act together and forgive herself for the sinful acts she's committed?" At these words, Claudia gazed at the floor, her face stricken with the appearance of uncertainty. "You're really willing to go down with the ship Charles?" Charles gave a slight nod. "I deserve what's coming for me Claudia. My fate is going to be sealed one way or another."

Charles began to walk out the door, leaving Claudia in an intense state of contemplation over a challenging conundrum. Before he exited, he looked back at Claudia. "Whatever you decide to do, make sure to do it before the Church event tomorrow afternoon." As Charles left the house, Claudia's little daughter, Meghan, began stealthily creeping downstairs, until she got on her mother's lap. Claudia continued to gently emit tears but laughed simultaneously as her daughter poked her nose. "Shouldn't you be asleep sweetie?" "I couldn't sleep with all that noise downstairs, mama." Claudia tried to smile as she looked into her daughter's beautiful light brown eyes. "Why are you sad mama? Are you gonna be okay?" Claudia utilized all the energy in her body to force a playful laugh. "Yes honey, everything's gonna go wonderfully!"

Charles gazed into his car window. It was beginning to rain heavily, dark clouds beginning to encompass the horizon, but he still wouldn't bring himself to go inside. Charles began to slam his face against the window, screaming with indignation. "What the fuck have I become?" He whispered to himself. He had become a demon spawned from hell, his moral compass shattered, his sense of dignity eradicated. His sister would be disgusted with the beast that he was. But this was the uncomfortable price that came with avenging her and now it was the price to possibly save Joshua.

Today's the Day
It was now eight a.m. in the morning. Today was the day Robert Wallace would make his unprecedented large donation to the Clairemont Church and hold one of the largest events the town has ever seen over it. Claudia spent the night attempting to write a proper confession letter addressing the heinous act she committed and exposing to the town that it wasn't a result of medical malpractice, but rather malicious and deliberate murder orchestrated by the highest echelons of local power. She solemnly kissed her children goodbye and headed towards the Clairemont Free Press to send her written confession. The Clairemont Free Press, contrary to its title, wasn't very free or independent. It was another propaganda wing of the town's establishment, but it was still the fairest paper of them all, even providing tepid criticisms of Wallace from time to time. Stricken with fear and uncertainty, she

swiftly placed her letter at the front desk of the press building and scurried out the building.

***

At the Clairemont Free Press meeting, ten a.m. that day, there was intense internal debate and discussion, the likes of which the organization had never seen prior. Everyone was fighting to convince the CEO, Patrick Longbottom, that their perspective on the recently sent letter, exposing the crimes of billionaire tycoon Robert Wallace, was correct. "Listen Matthew. The people have consolidated around Wallace now to a degree seldom seen prior. His announcement to send that ample sum of money to the Clairemont Church has created the perception that he's a benevolent billionaire being smeared by a cabal of satanists! This newspaper will do best if we cozy up to him." The man by the name of Matthew shook his head at the table and aptly responded to his coworker. "Our job is to be transparent and show the public the true face of what our power structures represent. Right now, Robert Wallace may be popular, but he is a paper tiger. As soon as we publish this bombshell, exposing the fact that he was in fact responsible for massacring an innocent grandmother, everybody, the elite and the masses, will turn on him and most important of all, this story will boost our paper's rating and wipe us clean of any legitimate local competition!"

The monologue about the virtues of journalism and exposing the true face of corrupt power structures bored CEO Patrick Longbottom. "Moralistic drivel," he thought to himself. But when Matthew mentioned the ratings this story would produce and the way it would wipe out the competition, his mind was made. And if the elite was inevitably going to turn on Wallace the paper didn't have to fear retribution, for the enemy would most likely be decapitated. CEO Patrick Longbottom finally found it fit to assert himself over the meeting. "We are going to publish this story! That's final." Longbottom gave a disingenuous grin. "Matthew is right. The public deserves to hear the truth about the fake human idols they're supposed to worship." Dismaying half the room, Longbottom turned to Matthew with a far more genuine grin this time. "Make sure to write the most punchy, merciless, and spellbinding newspaper article possible Matthew." The room reacted with mostly nods.

It was eleven thirty a.m. on this profound day. Joshua and Charles' plans to assassinate Robert Wallace did not require significant amounts of deliberation because it was relatively straightforward, perhaps to a fault. However, an inordinate amount of time was spent giving Joshua the proper makeover to assure that he wouldn't be recognized and fit in with the church crowd. He would dress and appear especially feminine to throw off people's perceptions and conceal his true identity. Charles noticed Joshua's peculiar fascination and engagement with his disguise. He seemed to revel in trying on makeup and lipstick, putting on a pretty white wig, and wearing high heels. It left Charles more bemused than disgusted. The event wouldn't start till five p.m. but Joshua was all dressed up and ready by one and seemed rather distracted by his dresswear. Still, Charles couldn't help but feel comforted by the joy emitting from Joshua's eyes and the relaxed sensations his body displayed for the first time in a long time.

At around 1:50 that day Charles got a call from Robert Wallace. He left his room to answer his soon to be deposed boss. Wallace began to deliver stunning news in a calm demeanor. "Do you see the headlines all over every news station and newspaper across this town? The nurse decided to open her ugly stinking mouth, Charles. Both you and I are in dark waters." Unbeknownst to Robert, Charles smiled. The best-case scenario had come true! Claudia decided to speak and apparently the papers decided to pick up her story.

"Sir, does this mean you're canceling the event today?" Before he even asked the question, he knew how Robert would answer. His arrogance was his most fatal flaw. "Hell no Charles! I'm gonna donate all that money to the Church and the masses will continue to love me for it. The show must go on!" Charles' smile grew even wider. "However, I'm gonna restrict Church attendance to the city's elite for now and they can each bring a maximum of two people with them." The call was silent for a moment. "Would that be all sir?" "No, actually. I need you to do something very important for me Charles." A deep and tormented chill began running through Charles' entire body.

"What would that be sir?" "I need you to take care of the Clairemont Free Press CEO and the nurse bitch who ratted us out. Can you execute my wishes before coming to the event, Charles?" Charles stood frozen for a moment. His entire body felt empty, and bereft of any will to continue moving. He finally replied. "It will be done sir." Charles ended the call before Wallace could further reply. He stared at the wall with utter contempt. It took all his energy and manpower to stop himself from slamming his face against the wall over and over again in sorrow and resignation.

***

Maximillian Wallace laid gently on a couch, rubbing his face against a pillow as his father spent the afternoon going through an assortment of different suits to try and figure out what to wear on this "splendid" day. "Are you afraid dad?" Robert turned towards his son. "What an asinine question boy. The police department still has my back. The town's elite have informed me in private that they have my back. The only ones who should be afraid are those drunkards, satanists and anarchists whispering about my inevitable collapse which will never come to pass!"

"Father?" "Yes son?" Maximillian paused for a moment to figure out how to articulate his thoughts in the most concise and inoffensive manner possible. "Why did you have to go so far? Why couldn't you simply drive Joshua out of town and let us live peacefully?" As he heard these words from his son. Robert's calm demeanor began to dissipate. His face began to simmer with intense expressions as he ripped the suit he was trying on off his body and approached Maximillian. Stricken with terror, Maximillian attempted to leave the couch, but his father grabbed him by the collar and spit on his face. "You UNGRATEFUL TWAT. I DID ALL THIS FOR YOU!

And this is how you repay me you fat, sniveling pig? You SPOILED BRAT!" Maximillian began pouting.

"But father, the kids at my school avoid me like the plague now. They treat me like a malignant disease. And the ones who do hang out with me, they hang out with me out of fear. All because of what you did! All because you murdered Joshua's grandmother!" Maximillian's father now gazed at him with his sympathetic eyes. It was the look his father typically displayed when he felt regretful for a particular action. Maximillian slowly approached his father but while he was expecting a hug, his father reached out and smacked his face. "I told you not to speak of this boy." Maximillian, now red in the face, and growing teary eyed, looked at his father with nothing short of pure animosity. "I'm not coming to your stupid event father. Maybe you can fuck a few more whores and you'll eventually get that good compliant son you always dreamed of."

At these words, Robert Wallace gave a look that signified nothing short of murderous intent. His first thought was to drag Maximillian by the collar and drag him to his room and then smack him with his own baseball bat till he was ready to be a good boy. Anticipating his father's actions, Maximillian swiftly dashed off the couch and ran towards the door. His father, quick for a man his size, grabbed his son's legs but Maximillian responded by elbowing his father on the face. Robert Wallace responded with a cry signifying utter pain and terror as his son ran off, too distant to capture. Robert Wallace sank to his knees and put his hands over his face, too ashamed to even show his tears to the face of nothingness.

***

Charles stood at the top of the Clairemont Free Press building. Entering through the front would inevitably produce a chaotic scene and wouldn't be surgical. Charles was sick and tired of killing, but there was a certain satisfaction to murdering the CEOs of press organizations.

Greedy low life's with loyalty to nothing but profiting off the suffering of townspeople. With stealth and subtlety, Charles exited the roof and entered the building's top floor. There at the far end stood the room of CEO Patrick Longbottom. What surprised him, however, was that he wasn't alone. Two private security guards hovered in front of the door, prepared to fire at any intruder.

Making sure not to be sighted, Charles quickly and quietly lunged behind a nearby pillar. He was a split second short of being caught by one of the guards. Panting intensely, he grabbed a Mask from his backpack and simultaneously grabbed a smoke can from his pocket and rolled it down the end of the hall. Before the security guards could even react or fire a bullet, the can began to emit heavy clouds of smoke and the guards collapsed. Suddenly the fire alarm began to go off and Charles burst with frustration. How could he forget to deactivate the fire alarm? "There goes avoiding a panic," he muttered to himself. Before Longbottom could run out of his room with the rest of the crew, Charles pulled out his pistol and barged into his room. Before Patrick Longbottom even had the opportunity to beg for his life, Charles shot him in the head.

Although the act of murder had often left Charles psychologically uncomfortable for hours on end, the grotesque headlines the Clairemont Free Press ran time after time, flashed through his mind, helping him assuage his guilt. A particularly pernicious headline from a few years back was vivid in Charles' mind. **CLAIREMONTS EPIDEMIC OF SLUTINESS**, it read. "Yea, this shit was deserved." he whispered to himself. The next victim Charles had to wipe out would be far more difficult to justify to himself. He was on the verge of leaving innocent children motherless.

***

Claudia spent prolonged periods of time looking out her window expecting to see cops at the front door to take her away. Or even worse, hired assassins. She had sent her children to high quality babysitters to avoid them from witnessing the potential chaos that would ensue at the premises of her home. Thus far she had witnessed a mob throw rocks at her and graffiti her property, and a few people walk by and spit on her lawn, but on this day, that was nothing compared to what could potentially happen. Claudia's phone rang. She had received a message from Charles. "Come meet by the town pier" it read. Claudia slowly put her phone back in her purse and froze.

It was finally time for her to meet her demise. She had dreamed of living a long, fruitful life watching her children grow and finding love once again. But that dream would soon dissipate, her corporeal self with it. There was no point in trying to run or hide. This was her fate.

The Clairemont town pier was a very pretty and modest area of the town. Fishermen often visited to catch the wide array of different fish that inhabited the lake. Of course, people seldom went swimming because the water was incomprehensibly chilly and cold. On this particular day, the pier and the entire lake area for that matter, was empty, bereft of the warm aura of humanity's playful endeavors. At the far end of the pier, Claudia noticed the outlines of Charles Hudson. Gazing at the ground for a moment, Claudia gulped, and began to approach her fate.

As Claudia approached him, Charles placed his hand on the holster of his firearm. He refused to look Claudia in the eyes. After a moment of pure silence, the sun's vibrant rays enclosing the two of them, Claudia began to slowly tear up. "Charles. Please just strike me down. Get this over with." Charles grabbed Claudia from behind and shoved her towards the edge of the pier. As she stood at the pier's edge, she gazed down at the calm waters and uttered the lord's name in desperation. Charles grabbed the gun from his holster and placed it on the center of Claudia's head. "You know I've spent most of my life reveling in sinful acts. Murdering in cold blood and justifying it to myself by invoking my sister and declaring my desire to cleanse this city a noble cause. Perhaps I'm a naive fool for what I'm about to do but it may open the gates toward a little bit of solace in my pathetic life." Claudia's terror-stricken fear had now transformed into confusion. Charles aimed the firearm away from the back of Claudia's face and right next to her ear. "Don't come back to this town anytime soon." Charles shot his gun into the air and pushed Claudia down into the shallow waters of the lake. As she floated on the lake's freezing waters, she smiled at the sun and ecstatically praised her lord.

Charles picked up his phone and called his employer. "I've eliminated them both sir."

***

There was only an hour remaining till the afternoon's cataclysmic event. Joshua looked out the window to the sight of protests more hostile and vigorous than the town had ever seen prior. Clairemont was already transformed into a battle ground as the sound of bullets rang through the streets, the significant power difference between the government troops and the townspeople did little to hinder the passionate yearnings for justice that permeated throughout the townspeople. As he witnessed buildings burning to the ground, and the city plunging itself into utter chaos, Joshua couldn't help but feel as though he was living inside a simulation. Not too long-ago Joshua was a nobody. The towns faggot that everyone and their grandmas avoided like the rabies, and yet here he was. He had inadvertently turned this town into a hellish landscape, simply by standing up to a school bully. Sometimes one person truly could make a difference.

As Joshua witnessed the turmoil that was encompassing the town, there was a loud knock on the door. But when he opened the door, he witnessed a sight he had never before seen. Charles had returned from his journey but the calm, resolute killer with an admirable temperament was gone. Instead, what Joshua saw was a fear-stricken man, his posture broken, and tears streaming down from his tired eyes. "Holy shit! Did something happen sir?" Charles said nothing and simply dragged himself towards the couch and collapsed in tears.

For approximately fifteen minutes, the room was devoid of any noise. One could hear a paper clip fall from the other corner of the universe without even a keen ear. As Charles began to speak, his voice no longer shone with the assertiveness and conviction that characterized it. "Joshua. You're such a lovely person. So, so lovely." Joshua gently touched Charles' forehead in concern. "I have come too far. I will make this town pay today; you will make it pay Joshua. But don't ever become like me. Don't let the monsters that roam Earth turn you into one." Joshua nodded. "I promise I will never become like them sir." The tears abruptly began to stop streaming down his eyes as Charles gazed into the ceiling in contemplation. "Joshua, I wanted to transform you into an instrument of destruction. I wanted you to become Nero himself. To make this callous species pay." Charles smiled. "But you deserve happiness. You deserve to live being who you are, not who others want you to be. And most of all, you deserve to love yourself. I'm so sorry." Joshua laid down on the couch next to Charles. It wasn't very comfortable due to the minimal space.

"Sir. Nobody has appreciated and respected me like you have. I will never forget what you've done for me, regardless of whether I die today or eighty years from now." "You know

Joshua, you'd make a very pretty girl." At this, Joshua lit up and gave a light giggle. "Thanks sir, although this dress is a little tight!"

***

Mayor Joseph Hellenburger sat down in front of a wide table with Chatalumas biggest entrepreneurs flickering and looking at him with utmost fear and concern. The mayor took a swig from his cup of whisky as he began to address the table. "I know you are all here today with utmost concern for the wellbeing of this great sprawling metropolis and business hub. But I assure you that everything will be under control!" The CEO of CyberSpace, the largest electronics provider for the city blurted out in disapproval. "You assured us that everything was under control a few days ago Mr. Mayor. Now we have communist insurgents popping up all over this city to rebel against our pro freedom privatization and union busting policies, inspired by the mayhem they saw in Clairemont!" Mayor Hellenburger chuckled, although it was clear his reaction was forced. "These commies are disorganized and disapproved of by the vast majority of this city! You have nothing to be concerned about sir. The police are cracking skulls and making sure to execute law and order! These degenerates will scurry away and disappear very soon."

"But how can you assure us that, when the city of Clairemont is on fire!" The CyberSpace CEO retorted. Others in the table began to nod resoundingly. The mayor gazed into his Whiskey for a moment and shrugged. "I warned Wallace to be responsible and intelligent. It's a pity that such a beautiful, Christ fearing town will soon likely degenerate into a hub for gambling and prostitution. But my intel indicates that the communists have no influence or control over Clairemont! The mafia will likely exploit the chaos and profit off of illegitimate businesses that will begin to pop up all over the chaotic town. And you boys can make ample profits by exchanging goods with them!" The entire table seemed to be satisfied with the answer given.

The mayor began to address the table with his own concerns. "Listen, if all of you patriotic CEOs and captains of industry want to continue profiting off of this town and making billions you need to help me stay popular. Make sure to keep the positive press coverage going, and sprinkle in a few light negative stories so they don't think the billionaires own the media or some silly shit Haha." Everyone at the table uniformly nodded. Joseph took one last final swig from his cup of Whisky. It seemed as though his throne was unshakable.

***

It was now approaching 4.50 p.m. While the Clairemont Church was typically a location exuding with beauty, the stained glass emanating with grandiosity as the sun's rays blaze upon it, and the stone pillars constructed with the same mastery as displayed in Roman architecture; the Church felt dreary and devoid of its typical charm. It was a militarized zone, with tanks and other vehicles surrounding the perimeter, attempting to hold the mass of protesters from breaking through the barrier. As Joshua and Charles stepped inside, in preparation for Robert Wallace's grand donation, they noticed that the interior was just as overwhelmed by security as the outside. As soon as they entered, officers patted them down to make sure they didn't carry weapons and as they began to take a seat in front of the magnificent tapestry, Joshua couldn't help but notice the police standing dispersed every few meters. He noticed a few men already seated, gazing at him peculiarly; they must've been turned on by his appearance, he thought amusedly.

Every few seconds, more people began to fill in the vacant seats. Members of the town elite, businessmen, church officials, government advisors etc. As the two of them sat in the middle row, waiting for Robert Wallace to arrive, Charles grabbed Joshua's shoulder. "Are you ready kid?" Joshua nodded. At that moment, the entire universe stood still. The noises that emanated from the room couldn't penetrate Joshua's consciousness. Every single moment of Joshua's life would climax at this precise moment. "This is for your grandmother," Joshua whispered to himself.

At approximately 5.02, Robert Wallace arrived at the scene, accompanied by the town's chief Pastor and the mayor. The audience rang out with applause, but Joshua noticed a sense of anxiety permeating from the crowd, the cheers tempered down from their typical vigor. A lot of the audience exchanged looks with one another, a sense of uncertainty outlined in their expressions. As the two other men sat down behind him, Robert Wallace took to the podium with an ignorant and out of place smile emanating from his face. "Hello, my fellow citizens of Clairemont," he announced with his booming voice.

"I want to start by thanking," Charles grabbed Joshua by the shoulder and began to whisper, "Now is the time child. Go use the bathroom." Joshua nodded and got up, but a nearby officer stopped him in his tracks. The officer gave Joshua a smile that suggested a form of respect. "Where are you heading to Ma'am?" The officer gently inquired as the speech continued.

Joshua tried to look the officer in his eyes. He had to make sure his voice was sufficiently feminine, or he'd be captured for certain. "I must use the bathroom," he gently squeaked. The officer smiled and gently nodded.

Joshua gave an immense sigh of relief as he continued towards the women's restroom. Joshua hurriedly entered the bathroom, kicked open the stall door, and grabbed the firearm from behind the toilet tank. He firmly placed the firearm in his dress pocket and headed out the door. Not a single cop interrogated Joshua as he rushed back to his seat. He briefly nodded towards Charles as Robert Wallace continued to drone on with his speech. Now Joshua had to find the most compelling time to interject and pull the trigger.

"Despite the lies propagated by phony media conglomerates and a loud and decadent minority, I stand strong and proud as a patriotic Christian." Joshua continued to notice how reluctant and perplexed the audience was, despite their applause as Wallace spoke. His rhetoric clearly wasn't having the same effect it once had. "Due to my absolute loyalty to God and the people of this town, I will now write a check donating 1 billion dollars to Clairemont Church!" As the Church rang with applause, Robert Wallace grabbed a pen from his pocket and revealed a checkbook to the crowd. He waved his hands, indicating to the audience his permission to allow them to settle down. He quickly wrote his signature and a sum of money onto the check and began waving it in the air to indicate his massive donation. He then turned to the chief pastor and handed him the check as the waves of applause reached their crescendo.

Joshua couldn't believe the cowardly seals that populated the building. A tinge of pessimism had emanated from within himself. Robert Wallace walked back towards the podium to begin speaking once again. "I have spent my entire life serving the cause of social justice. To protect the most vulnerable people in our society, just as Christ did." At these words, Joshua began to fume. His pessimism and withdrawn attitude transformed into a boiling anger, a desire to explode in utter contempt. He knew it was time. Joshua burst out from his seat to the absolute astonishment of everyone surrounding him and screamed. "YOU LYING SON OF A BITCH. YOU KILLED MY GRANDMOTHER. YOU MURDERED HER IN COLD BLOOD. AND YOU'RE GONNA PAY FOR IT."

Before Robert Wallace could begin to smooth talk his way out of the situation, Joshua pointed his gun right between the billionaire's two eyes and pulled the trigger. At that moment it was absolute pandemonium as the bullet hit Wallace's forehead, splattering blood all over the tapestry and the town's elite began dashing towards the exits. Charles, however, stood by Joshua, holding him by the shoulder. Meanwhile, a couple meters away, the mass of protesters had managed to penetrate the perimeter established by military units and began to storm into the Church building. Windows were shattered, and virtually every inch was left scathed as baseball bats and cocktail bottles were used to smash up the building.

The police were on the verge of opening fire at Joshua and Charles, but the mob, roaring to life, had surrounded the two of them in a protective posture, refusing to break ranks. The officers looked to one another with perplexity and decided ultimately to fire through the entire crowd, but the town's Mayor stopped them. "You buffoons! Have you not read a history book? Open fire and the victims will become martyrs and we will collapse with certainty!" The officers put their firearms back into their holsters as the crowds cheered with visceral passion. "The hoards have won this day. Evacuate the building officers!" The mayor stated with a firm but disgruntled tone.

Robert Wallace's dead body laid bleeding on the tapestry floor, alone and rotting. Charles gazed into the abyss of emptiness, his surroundings intoxicated by the pure joy and temporary destruction of the established order. "I've done this for you sister. I've made this town pay for what it did to you." As Charles slowly began to exit the premises of the Church, he noticed the dead bodies of the town elite, dispersed across the floor, butchered in the most unspeakably heinous of ways. Heads detached from their bodies, spines ripped out and broken to pieces. Yet this gruesome carnage was insignificant compared to all the disobedient women, queers, and non-believers this town ostracized and left to slowly decay in misery and subjugation. Charles had fulfilled his duty, although it pulled him into the fiery pits of self-loathing and unquenched guilt, in the process.

Reckoning

Clairemont Police Chief Peter Tool looked at Mayor Douglas Harrison with utter revulsion. "Why didn't you let my men open fire on that terrorist scumbag Mr. Mayor? Why did you let the satanic cabal lay waste to our magnificent place of worship?" The mayor gave an expression of disbelief at the Police Chiefs question, as if he was dealing with an absolute buffoon. "If we opened fire at a mass of people protesting the extrajudicial killing of an old lady, orchestrated by the highest echelons of power, our credibility would diminish even further, officer!" The mayor subtly peeked out the window from Town Hall. There continued to be protests dispersed throughout the town, and the grounds were laid waste by the conflict that shook the polity to its core, but things were tempering down.

"The only thing these homosexual rebel clowns understand is the terror of the baton and the power of our bullets sir." The mayor held back his laughter. "Have you bothered to take a sociology, psychology, or history class, officer? Because absolutely nothing you have stated is borne out by the shit that's actually gone down! We tried the tough on crime approach, the shoot 'em up approach, and look where it got us!" "But" "No buts! You do as I order, or I will use all my political capital to ostracize you and make sure you never hold a major position again, you hot headed cock sucker." The officer reluctantly nodded, although his facial expressions indicated a contrary feeling of pure animosity.

***

Giddy and trembling with excitement, Joshua entered the premises of Charles' apartment room, unsure how to display his gratitude and express thanks to the man. But what he saw when he entered the room was profoundly heart stopping and unexpected. The dead body of Joshua's former European history teacher laid there on the ground with a look of dissatisfaction appearing on his frozen face. A bottle of pills was open, lying there next to him, and a pistol held in his sweaty palms. The floor was soaking with blood pouring out of a bullet hole punctured on the sides of his head. Joshua shook his head in utter disbelief, and disorientation. "No! No! Sir? Come back please. I need you sir." Joshua fell to his knees next to a man who stood as a late father figure to him and burst out in tears. "I was supposed to die. Not you. Not you." Grimacing, Joshua gently laid there next to Charles' body.

There was an envelope placed on Charles' chest. Joshua

was reluctant to pick it up. Every time he had uncovered a new piece of information in his life, it shattered his fragile soul, inch by inch. After breathing heavily and laying there in disbelief for thirty minutes, Joshua ultimately decided to pick up the envelope. Located inside was a letter, smeared with tears. Rubbing the tears against his hands, Joshua began to read the letter...

Joshua, my dear child. I know you've looked up to me as a patron saint and father figure. A paragon of strength and excellence. But I must regretfully shatter that perception with a difficult dose of reality. I was a brutal murderer. A thug. A pawn to my own primitive desire for vengeance. I told myself I did it for Gazebella, but I did it to satisfy my most primal desires. And I hurt you too. Before I go, I want to write this letter to make you aware that I murdered your grandmother. I regret it, like I regret most of my actions. But I know regret will never bring that innocent woman back to life. I am sorry Joshua, please don't look too harshly at me when I inevitably enter your memory as a ghost of your tumultuous past. I'm Sorry Joshua.

Joshua gazed at the letter in absolute silence for a moment. It couldn't be. How could life be so cynical and twisted? It just couldn't be true. But it was. Joshua ripped the note to pieces and began stomping on the floor in absolute disbelief. He screamed into the ether, begging for God to hold him in his lap and assure him it was all just a cruel and cynical little dream. But it wasn't. It was reality. Joshua's greatest mentor, the man who meant the universe to him, murdered the only woman who ever truly loved him. Joshua hid his face in his palms, and cried in utter discontent and revulsion, unfortunately without a father to comfort his lost soul.

***

Mayor Douglas Harrison looked at his approval ratings with astonishment. Even as the town continued to reckon with the terror engulfing it in its preceding days, and the terror that continued to engulf it, over forty percent of the population still approved of the job he was doing. Video footage of him restraining the police from murdering the mob went viral and he was commended for his sense of virtue. Of course, his actions were a cynical political gambit to preserve the institutions that maintained the town's coherence, but it didn't matter. He had to make sure the upcoming trial of Joshua McCarthy wouldn't plunge this town further down a path of inescapable turmoil.

Judge Pierce Broman entered the office of the mayor, and respectfully nodded at Mayor Harrison. "You have summoned me sir?" "Yes, Judge, I want you to do something of massive significance for me. It's illegal that I summon you here to discuss this topic, but I know you put the citizens of this town before anything else." The Judge nodded. "There will inevitably be a trial and that boy, Joshua, will be found guilty by a jury of his peers. He murdered Wallace in front of countless eyewitnesses and there's little ambiguity on that front." As if for dramatic effect, the mayor stood up as he continued to speak. "However, I'm gonna need you to give as light a sentence as possible for the boy."

The Judge stared blankly towards the mayor. "But sir, not only is this a breach of conduct and the sacrosanct principle of an impartial trial, it would also incentivize rebellion amongst the public!" The mayor nodded in agreement. "This would be a breach of the sacrosanct values that the court system is predicated on, yes. But remember, judge, that there may be no court system left to uphold if these riotous masses sense an aura of injustice. And we both know what Robert Wallace did to that boy. What he did to many others without ever being held accountable."

The judge sat in contemplation for a moment; he had experienced countless moral conundrums in his career, but none so challenging. "Listen, Mr. Broman, this is your decision. You are the arbiter of justice. I just ask that you consider what hangs in the balance." The judge stared at the wall, transfixed.

***

Joshua found his trial to be the most humiliating experience in his life. After pleading guilty, Joshua's government appointed lawyer attempted to portray the narrative that he was mentally ill and thus unfit for either prison or capital punishment. Testimony after testimony was delivered describing Joshua's peculiar and "homosexual" tendencies, it seemed as though his lifestyle was more on trial than the actual murder, he committed. Of course, Joshua accepted this strategy because living out the rest of his life in a mental health facility was vastly preferable to the alternatives. At one point, his lawyer asserted, "Joshua literally wore a dress when he committed the murder for Christ's sake!", which made Joshua snicker a little bit. Joshua didn't have much experience with courts, but he nonetheless found the Judge's behavior to be quite peculiar. It seemed as though he wasn't even paying attention to the ongoing trial, likely contemplating about some fantasy land, and arbitrarily decided which objections to sustain and overrule.

When the verdict was ultimately declared however, Joshua fell into a state of utter disbelief. He wasn't given the death penalty, life in prison, or even a single year in prison for that matter. The judge had determined that Joshua would be sentenced to spend time in the "Chataluma mental health facility until he was cured of his disorderly behavior." Joshua's attorney was absolutely ecstatic about this declaration, hugging Joshua tightly at this news. However, the decision left Joshua in a state of intense contemplation about how he could possibly receive such a light sentence.

Moments after the sentencing, Joshua was knocked out, blind folded and dragged away into a vehicle headed for Chataluma.

"Therapy"

It was his first morning at the Chataluma mental health facility, Joshua sat alone in his tiny room, rubbing his eyes and yawning. Prior to the morning, at midnight Joshua was forced to strip naked and shower in front of officers and given blue scrubs to put on. Unfortunately, it was impossible for him to get proper sleep because the doors were left open every five minutes and workers would check on him with a flashlight that emitted the most intense glare Joshua had ever witnessed.

It was announced that breakfast was ready, so Joshua headed towards the kitchen a few meters away from his room. Much to his disappointment, the food offered was either a half slice of French toast or cereal with the choice of apple juice or milk for drinks. "This hellhole doesn't even have orange juice," Joshua uttered to himself in dismay. After quickly scarfing down his French toast, Joshua hurried back to his room. There were supposed to be sessions commencing for the patients in the activity room, but Joshua simply refused to participate. A counselor informed Joshua that the more activities he engaged in, the sooner he would leave. This however did little to sway Joshua's mind. As dissatisfying as this ward was, nothing existed for Joshua in the outside world. He would be a nobody, scampering around to survive rather than truly live. Besides, Joshua knew he had done nothing wrong. If he didn't murder Wallace, Wallace would've murdered him.

As Joshua laid his head against his pillow, pondering whether his grandmother was up in heaven with the magnificent angels, a young female counselor with long black hair approached his room. "The psychiatrist would like to speak to you sir." "Do I have to see them?" The counselor nodded. Sighing heavily, Joshua left his room and followed the counselor to the end of the hall.

***

A black man with large spectacles and a stern demeanor gazed at Joshua as he took a seat.

There was an uncomfortable look of pity and disgust in the man's eyes, and Joshua instantly knew what kind of therapeutic session this would be. "Good evening, Joshua. I, along with the social workers and counselors here are tasked to help you improve your mental state and become a proper citizen." Joshua held back his urge to display a sarcastic tone and nodded. "Thank you." One would think that an individual convicted of murder would be getting therapy sessions to help mitigate his homicidal impulses, but as subsequent moments would prove, one would be wrong.

"So, Joshua my papers here inform me that you're a closeted homosexual?" Joshua grinned. "Yea, sure dude." The therapist shook his head with a look of immense concern. "Joshua, our staff here at the Chataluma mental health facility will do our utmost to repress your homosexual urges and prevent you from murdering again!" Now Joshua had to use his utmost energy to repress the laughter that was ready to explode within him at any moment. "Thank, thank you very much sir." Suddenly, Joshua's mind lit up with a bright idea. He would pretend to be a homosexual and as soon as he was bored of this shithole, he would suddenly declare he lost his homosexual urges and be released! "Brilliant, bloody brilliant," Joshua thought to himself in amusement.

 The psychiatrist continued, unfazed by Joshua's reactions. "I understand the struggle of living with degenerative and deviant thoughts Joshua. I have a son who dealt with similar sinful attitudes he was forced to wrestle with. Luckily, he came out cured and better than ever!" Joshua, deciding it would be quite amusing, began to pretend he was pouting in sorrow.

 "But-but sir, do you think I will ever be cured of these dirty thoughts? I'm very nervous. I see a penis and I know Satan is penetrating my mind, but I can't help finding it so enticing." Unaware of the comedic routine Joshua was engaging with, the psychiatrist grabbed Joshua's shoulder and looked him firmly in the eyes. "Listen, son, I understand it's difficult to wrestle with the demonic forces that penetrate our psyche. But I promise you that the team here will cleanse your mind of the darkness and you will be free from both the sexually perverse and homicidal thoughts that have left you in such harrowing pain." Joshua nodded, suppressing the amusement that flickered within him. "Thank you very much sir." "Oh, it's my pleasure Joshua. Now, have a wonderful and healthy rest of your day buddy!"

***

Joshua tried to sleep through the morning, a time where there wouldn't be flashlights burning his eyes every five minutes. Ironically, Joshua hated sleep time when he was five or six years old but as he got older, he appreciated the solemnity and peace that manifested in the period of rest more and more. Unfortunately, this time around, his rest would be cut short. As Joshua experienced a vivid dream, with his grandmother sprouting butterfly wings and riding him through the mountains, two of the facility workers grabbed Joshua by his legs and dragged him to the group activities, his body smearing against the germ ridden floors in the process.

The sight of Joshua made everyone at the activity room howl with laughter and mockery.

There were numerous eccentric and distinct personalities in the room. The counselor attempted to get everyone's attention but upon the commotion and recklessness exhibited, there was no hope. One guy was slamming his face against the table every two seconds, in fact his head slamming seemed to operate with a certain rhythmic pattern. Two girls were pulling at each other's hair, clearly distraught at one another. It would require endless paragraphs of highly descriptive language to further convey the utter madness of what was on display.

However, as Joshua got up from the ground, shaking off the agitation he felt after his serene period of sleep was disturbed, he witnessed a girl at the corner of the room, her head resting against the window. She had long and curly brown hair, a tattoo displaying a half moon etched onto her neck and illuminating black eyes that particularly resonated with Joshua. Attempting to be subtle and respectful, Joshua slowly sat nearby the girl and pretended to look elsewhere. But he noticed the girl smile. "What do you want, weirdo?" Joshua turned and looked her in the eyes. "So, you noticed me." The girl nodded. "Yea, I'm used to creepy guys trying to hit on me. I can sense it from a mile away." The girl continued to rest her head against the window as she spoke.

Joshua vehemently shook his head. "No, I promise that's not what I'm trying to do. I just wanted to get to know you, that's all." "Right. Okay. Well, my name is Claire Darling." "I'm Joshua." Claire's eyes turned wide. "No fucking way! You're that kid who shot the billionaire bloke!" Joshua laughed. "Indeed. Looks like my reputation precedes me. But how the fuck did you even know that?" Claire giggled. "Trust me cowboy, I have my ways of getting info around here."

"You know Joshua, you really shouldn't even be here. The mentally incompetent thing to do would be letting the mother fucker who killed your grandmother loose." Joshua decided not to answer. Part of him felt uncomfortable lingering on the past events that unfolded in his life. "So, Claire. How did you get here?" "If I tell you, I hope you won't judge me too harshly for it Joshua." Joshua's heart sank for a moment. Was he talking to some homicidal maniac or mass rapist or pedophile? Joshua shook his head. "Don't worry Claire, it's not my place to judge you."

"Well, my life was a relatively simple and stable one. I had a loving relationship with my upper middle-class parents and I was studying for my bachelor's in computer science. I was volunteering for a homeless shelter at the time, and I fell in love with the most unexpected of people. She was a homeless Hispanic girl whos' adoptive parents abandoned her without leaving a cent, cuz she was too peculiar for them, a freak."

"The thing is, Joshua, I'm a freak too. I repressed it in the name of getting honors, being loved by my community, and having a healthy relationship with my supportive family. But this girl I met, I could be open with her. My most intimate desires, my true identity, I could reveal myself in a way I never could to anybody else. I could talk to her about lesbian vampires, hot girls, my favorite queer bands!" Claire gave a serene smile, exuding with a sense of longing. "We fell in love. I dropped out of school and decided to invest all my energy in finding work to support her.

"Unfortunately, my parents discovered that the two of us were together. She became hysterical, told me she couldn't believe God had punished her with such a deceitful and sick daughter. And she reported me to the authorities for having an unclean relationship." For the first time since they had met, Claire looked Joshua in the eyes, a tortured sense of emptiness exuding from her eyes. "I don't know where she went. With me gone, she likely gave into her crack addiction and disappeared forever."

Joshua gently patted Claire's shoulders. "It was very brave of you to tell me these things." "I have no idea why I even told you all of that. I suppose I see a bit of myself in you?" Joshua cracked a smile. "Oh, I'm absolutely a freak!" "God, I just wish I could get the fuck out of this hellhole and search for her." Joshua looked at Claire with a puzzled expression. "Don't you fear the misery and emptiness that lurks out there? The cynicism of the streets that plunge you into a state of utter hostility and fatalistic resignation?" Claire's enigmatic black eyes now penetrated Joshua's consciousness as she looked at him with certitude. "I may suffer the moment I get out there in the real world. I may drown in a pool of blood as a psychotic mob slowly pummels me to death in the streets. But I would rather spend my time aimlessly searching for that spark of love, then rot here underneath the pressures of institutional lies, of centuries of superstitious traditions trying to convince me that I'm wrong in the head for loving someone different from the rest of the herd."

Joshua slowly began to tear up for the first time in a long while. "But I'm afraid, Claire. I was born a curse upon my own family, and every day I live out there I begin drowning upon the slow and dreadful realization that God seeks to punish me and burn to ashes any resemblance of sanity I still have." Claire squeezed Joshua's hands tightly, as she also began tearing up. "Joshua, life can be dreadful, it feels easy to resign yourself to the dictates of institutional gatekeepers. It makes you feel safe and cozy and free from the horrors of the world. Hell, free from the pleasure and joy that you know will diminish sooner or later. But that pain and pleasure makes you human. I may sound like a cliche bitch, but do you really want to forgo the extravagances of life to live a safe and monitored lie?"

Joshua's head was thumping with disarray and abject confusion. He didn't want to suffer another blow by the hands of fate, but so many had sacrificed their lives so he could truly live.

"Thank you so much Claire."

PART III

Disgraced

"You swore allegiance to law and order when you put on this badge and you have betrayed your duties and disgraced our institution Mr. Nelson." Chatalumas police commissioner, Randall Cunningham, looked at now ex officer Pierre Nelson with utter contempt in his eyes. "I trusted you! I treated you like a brother. When your ex-wife tried to report you for beating her to a pulp, I used my power and capital to make sure you'd be safe from investigation. And this is how you repay me Nelson? By disobeying an order and putting our boys at risk?"

Pierre Nelson was a highly decorated and respected officer for the city of Chataluma. He had done an effective job putting countless murderers, rapists, robbers, and communists behind bars. But he was now officially stripped of his position and likely never to receive a role in law enforcement again. All because he refused to follow the Police chief's grotesque order. He had no idea why he stopped complying at that moment, why he chose to grow a spine precisely then and refuse orders, but he did. He was instructed to shoot and kill a black man who escaped his grip and began running away from the police vehicle.

The black man was arrested under suspicion of having membership in the communist party and was a prime suspect for terror operations that wreaked havoc throughout the city.

But at that moment. Pierre couldn't pull the trigger and end that miserable son of a bitch's life. Years of carrying out orders, committing sin in the name of justice, and having a parade of naive fools celebrating you and treating you like a paragon of virtue. He couldn't do it at that moment, continue the cycle, and a man evaded arrest because of it. Of course, upon hearing of Pierre's insubordination, the authorities were almost ubiquitously left in a state of disbelief. The man who engaged in countless unethical operations, planting fake evidence, shooting unarmed suspects, lying to save his fellow officers. They all pondered the same question. Why the sudden transformation?

Pierre couldn't answer that question himself. He was uncertain what went into him, why his consciousness panged at that very moment. But it didn't matter. He had made the decision he made, and there was no turning back. He had to begin reforming himself. Leave the ways of the officer and become a true beacon of justice. But now he was an absolute nobody. The equivalent of a hobo.

Pierre decided to visit a bar at the outskirts of Chataluma. It was midnight but the city never slept and most of it permeated with raunchy music, an assortment of bright and flashy colors, tourists and residents alike flooding stores to buy an endless supply of commodities, and waves of protesters espousing a plethora of different ideological perspectives. The outskirts were far more serene and peaceful than the rest of the city and Pierre desperately needed that at the moment. Purchasing a locally brewed beer, Pierre sat down at a corner of the bar, and gazed up at the ceiling in dismay. What was he even supposed to do now? His life was fundamentally purposeless, and his body would soon become an empty vessel. As he took a swig from his beer, Pierre knew he needed a miracle.

After taking a few more swigs, Pierre got up, tipped the bartender $five, and exited the bar. The taste of sweet beer typically mitigated Pierre's emotional turmoil but it wasn't very effective this time around. As he headed outside, Pierre noticed two officers harassing a young black boy in front of a SUV. With ease and subtlety, Pierre stealthily rushed behind a nearby red truck, a few feet from the SUV, to eavesdrop into the conversation.

"Kid, I don't give two shits about your sob story. Whichever one of my boys shot down your mother probably did it because she was a despicable nigga. Now apologize for calling me a pig right now or I'll give you a beating like you've never seen before." The moment he registered what the officer said, Pierre heard enough. He pulled the firearm out of his holster and fired two bullets, each one aimed at the two officers' hats. His aim was as sharp as ever, and both the police caps fell from the officer's head. Without ever so slightly attempting to retaliate the two officers dashed to their police car and fled the scene in an instant. "Cowards." Pierre muttered in satisfaction. The boy began to walk away from the spot of the confrontation, but Pierre leaped out from behind the red truck and confronted him.

"Look kid, you can just walk away and try to avoid another unpleasant meeting with the cops.

"But you won't last long. They're blood thirsty and always prepared to finish where they left off bullying civilians that piss them off. If you come with me, I can help protect you." The boy turned reluctantly to look at Pierre. He appeared to be no older than thirteen years old, with a bald head, and larger than average eyebrows. "My name is Pierre. At your service kid."

***

Pierre took the boy with him to his poorly ventilated and subpar apartment room. He wouldn't utter a word on the way there. Pierre wasn't an expert in psychology but he had seen enough traumatized individuals throughout his time as an officer to understand that this kid had been through the wringer one too many times. Pierre rummaged through his refrigerator until he found a can of baked beans for the child and decided to confront him in the kitchen. "Listen kid, I'm here to help you out. You can stay with me as long as you need to but if we're gonna do this you have gotta at least tell me something. Like… what's your name?"

To Pierre's surprise the boy finally spoke up, but it wasn't to answer his question. "You still aren't married? I mean you look pretty old." For a moment, Pierre frowned, but the frown dissipated and was quickly replaced by snickers. The boy began to laugh with him. "No kid, I ain't married. I was but then I chose to be an insufferable twat and absolute asshole." Pierre gazed at the table, embarrassed to look the boy in his eyes.

"Listen, kid, if you ever want to keep those you love around you forever, remember to always listen. You might think you're right, you may wanna be the boss, but you ain't." The boy's response plunged Pierre into a deeper state of guilt. "Oh, trust me, I know a man just like you. My goddamn papa." Pierre forced himself to gaze into the boy's sharp brown eyes. "I'm sorry kid, I imagine that truly sucked." The boy shook his head. "Why you apologizing? You aren't my father!" Pierre could feel the boy's intense inner turmoil from across the table and did something he would've considered "pussy" and "emasculate" a few months ago. He reached across the table and held onto the boy's hands.

"My papa would always pester my mother. Why didn't you make this food the exact way I wanted it! Why can't you ever listen to my commands like a mom's supposed to! Why are you spoiling the boy with your bitchy love?" Pierre squeezed the child's hand tighter, shamefully, he couldn't help but notice the resemblance between the boy's father and himself. "Eventually my father dumped my mother to go have a relationship with some car saleswoman he ran into. Left us both forever." Tears began to flow down the boy's eyes. Gently rubbing them off his face, he continued.

"My mother was devastated. She had no idea where to go. Our food stamp benefits were slim, and she told me she needed supplemental income. I wasn't sure exactly what kind of work she was gonna be up to, but I had an idea. One day, as the two of us exited the local barber, two of them pigs confronted us. One of them tried to pull me away from the scene but I wouldn't budge. My mother tried to dash from the scene but instead of trying to capture her, both the officers sprayed." The boy paused for a moment, "sprayed her with bullets." The boy now burst with tears. Pierre awkwardly tried to comfort him, but it was no use. He was now certain of one thing, however. He couldn't tell this boy about who he was, the true monster within. Because the things Pierre did, the way he terrorized the marginalized, made the action's the boy described almost seem like kid's play.

One thing was certain, however. Pierre couldn't simply drown in tears of self-pity, agonizing over the monstrosities he was responsible for. He had to actively spend his days on Earth trying to make up for the vile actions he was complicit and responsible for. As the boy continued to tear up in utter agony,

Pierre stood up. "Listen kid. I know this might sound batshit crazy but what if I teach you how to fight. Help you fend off against those pigs on your own." Although the tears continued to sprinkle from his eyes, Pierre noticed the boy light up a little bit. The boy slowly began to nod, and Pierre knew this was the perfect opportunity to ask the question that was burning within him.

"But kid, if we're gonna be partners, we have got to know each other at least a little bit. So...what's your name?" The boy gave a wide, cheery smile. "My name is Xavier."

Back to Life

Over the next couple of days, Joshua began to contemplate exiting the psyche ward. All he could really do in the facility was sleep, walk around in circles, drink decaffeinated coffee, and play board games. The psyche ward had certainly improved his mental health, making life vastly simpler by eliminating all the uncertain variables that plagued him in the real world, but he needed more. While he feared the volatile outside world and all the possible nasty surprises that were yet to await him, Claudia's love story couldn't help but leave an impression, deeply etched into his mind. Perhaps, there was an unfound purpose in his life, or a spark of love waiting to rejuvenate him and make life worth living. Either way, he wouldn't ever find out if he was stuck in this hole.

Although reluctant to leave, Joshua dropped the act of being a homosexual (as amusing as it was), and suddenly declared himself cured. The social workers, shockingly enough, bought it. They likely felt so affirmed that their conversion therapy methods were effective that they let the obvious slip right in front of them. Joshua originally planned on breaking out with Claudia, hoping she too could find that spark she desired so heavily, but Claudia refused. "I'm not running from these homophobic bastards," she would assert.

***

The moment he was freed from the ward, Joshua collapsed into a state of absolute despair. The city of Chataluma was simply incomparable to where he grew up in Clairemont. As he walked the streets, greens, blues, purples, and various other colored lights flashed before his eyes, as thousands of people scurried off to countless destinations. Skyscrapers pierced the night sky as Joshua gazed upwards and as he looked back down, an endless assortment of stores intimidatingly stood in front of him, a sight incomprehensible to the boy who grew up in a simple Christian town.

Nearby, Joshua noticed a trash can, and quickly dashed to it and began to heavily barf. He noticed passerby's giving concerned looks towards his direction as he queasily returned to the sidewalk paths, puzzled at what to possibly do. As he walked the streets he noticed homeless men, women, and children begging for crumbs, and people giving them stern and disgusted looks in response. One mother dragged her five-year-old child away from a homeless man playing his guitar for people passing by. The reactions left Joshua in a state of utter revulsion. These were probably the same degenerates who forced both his fathers to hide their identities.

There were so many options in the city, music halls, pizza shops, magic shows, museums, but Joshua didn't have cash on him, and he didn't find anything particularly to his liking anyways.

He finally decided on entering a robot themed bar, despite being incapable of purchasing anything there. The waiters at this peculiar joint seemed to be box shaped robots who moved around in wheels and held the plates with their awkwardly shaped hands, poorly strung to their bodies.

Joshua took a seat at a table at the distant corner of the bar, ready to sulk away in abject misery. However, as he began to be consumed by thought, a voice he had never before heard wrung in his ears. "Joshua? Holy shit, is that you!" As he looked up, Joshua became even more bewildered than prior. In front of him was a goth girl with light brown eyes, very pale skin, long and smooth black hair, and tons of makeup. She was wearing a short skirt, long white socks, and a T-shirt with lots, and lots of skulls. Her voice however seemed to emanate with a more masculine aura. Attempting to make sense of the ecstatic reaction this random girl had at seeing Joshua, he decided to question her. "Soooooo…uhhhhhh, do I know you mam?"

The girl seemed to laugh at his question. "Joshua! You basically saved me from getting my ass beat by that Maximillan kid!" At that moment, Joshua froze in absolute disbelief. "No, it can't be," he whispered. "Yeaaa, I got a bit of a makeover and all that. How do you like my new look Joshie?" Joshua couldn't fathom what he saw before him. It wasn't exactly long ago when he saw that young boy, stricken with terror, defenseless and on the verge of being beaten to a pulp by the school's most vicious bully. Joshua's intervention at the time completely changed the trajectory, not just of his life, but the entire town. But now that same child stood in front of him, in a completely distinct form.

The girl took a seat next to Joshua, sipping her lemonade as he gazed at her in a transfixed state. "Look, Joshua, what you did in our old town, it changed so many of our lives. And it especially changed me." Joshua nodded. "I deeply apologize." "No, silly, you shouldn't be apologizing, I should be thanking you actually." These words caught Joshua by absolute surprise. "What do you mean by that?" "Look, Joshua. Clairemont forced us all to be inauthentic people, actors to make our families and rulers happy. I never wanted to be a shy, little boy who went to church on Sunday's and did my chores and got good grades for my mommy and daddy. Always feeling guilty to jerk off because apparently having sex with yourself is a sin!" At this comment, Joshua burst out laughing.

"Nah, I didn't want to have my hair short, and wear respectable clothing, and pretend to be something I wasn't. I wanted to be a punk bad ass girl ya know? And you finally gave me the spark to dump all that bullshit and live a new and authentic life! I shaved off my leg hairs, got a long wig, started trying on all sorts of makeup, and wearing clothes I actually felt comfortable in. I decided to be independent, make my own dough if you get what I'm saying dude! I dumped my parents and decided to come to the big city!" Hearing her story, Joshua couldn't help but feel reaffirmed that he did the right thing, and more certain than ever that he would've confronted Maximillian again if he could.

"So, how is this whole being independent thing going for you?" At this question, the girl seemed to give a hesitant smile. "Well, Joshua, to tell you the truth it's a bit hard and all, but overall, it's going wonderfully!" Joshua felt very skeptical of what he heard, and it was clear she didn't want to further elaborate, so the two of them awkwardly sat there for a minute. "So, what's your name!" "My name is Joanna Andersen!" "Very cool. Did you have a name before that?" Joanna frowned at the question. "Joshua! You're not supposed to ask a transgirl what her dead name was! That's terrible manners!" "Oh, shit, I'm so fucking sorry Joanna. I really didn't mean to cause harm; I apologize for my ignorance."

Joanna began to glow. "Aww Joshua, don't worry about it. The fact that you reacted to criticism in such a mature way makes you so different from most guys. You know that?" Joshua nodded hesitantly. Similar to how he often felt recently, Joshua experienced a certain discomfort at being called a guy, but he couldn't fully admit to himself why. "You know Joshua, this is going to sound very embarrassing but I always thought of myself as a lesbian. But the moment I laid my eyes on you, I began to become skeptical of that." The moment Joshua registered these words into his mind, he sprinted. He dashed through the doors and ran and ran some more.

Lights and brand logos flashed past his eyes, various horns and the noises of the sleepless city night rang in his ears, and the bitter cold subsumed his body, but he kept running. His mind was an empty fog, and he couldn't pinpoint why but his instincts told him to keep on running.

He finally stopped as he witnessed a magnificent lake in front of him, an ice cream cart at the corner of the sidewalk. The area was engulfed by seagulls fighting for bread thrown at them by a crowd of bird watchers. As Joshua panted heavily, he couldn't even begin to fathom what was going on inside his mind. Why did he sprint on sight the moment a girl began to confess her admiration for him? Isn't this what he always wanted? To be appreciated? But actually, hearing those words of admiration out loud, especially from such a beautiful girl, it felt too good to be true. But it was real, and he lost it now. That possible chance to finally find love. Be with someone who could perhaps even understand him. Joshua stomped his legs in absolute anger. "WHAT THE FUCK IS WRONG WITH MEEEEEEEEEEE." "Hey, dude, what's the matter?" Joshua turned around, and almost fainted on sight, but quickly held himself together.

"How the fuck did you find me?" "I chased you down, silly goose, didn't you hear the footsteps?" Joshua, continuing to pant intensely, and gently shook his head. "I'm sorry Joanna, I'm so sorry for running away like that." "I know you're sorry Joshua, I'm sorry for throwing that out there so randomly! Must have been terrifying." Side by side, the two of them gazed out at the lake, a gentle breeze slapping against their faces. Joanna reached out and grabbed Joshua's hands, it seemed as though a spark was truly lit.

Vengeance

Xavier panted heavily as he looked up at Pierre. "How many more times do I gotta run this entire field dude?" "Until I tell you to stop;" Xavier rolled his eyes. "Bruh! When you recruited me to learn how to fight those pigs, I thought you'd be teaching me kung fu, and shit. Or how to shoot a gun like a pro?" Pierre smiled. "You're literally making the same complaints every student makes in the movies and shows. Quit being so cliche Xavier! I know you know that physical strength is essential to being a fearsome warrior." Xavier reluctantly nodded and began to run another lap.

After a few days of arduous physical training, which involved many trips to the gym and many laps across the field, Xavier was excited to learn what he deemed the "bad ass shit." Xavier was a rapid learner, quickly comprehending the basics of firearms training, and shooting his targets with phenomenal precision. It left Pierre stunned, considering it took him months to shoot as well as Xavier could in less than a week. Towards the end of the week, Pierre took Xavier hunting. He observed that the boy was naturally stealthy and deeply focused. Before the day ended, he managed to shoot a deer in the head right between its two eyes.

One fine evening, the two of them completed their training early and decided to visit a nearby grocery store to pick up food for the weekend. Before the two of them could make it inside however, Pierre ran into a familiar face. He tried to hurry inside before he was spotted but it was too late. "Pierre! How's retirement been, man?" There stood officer Jonathan Doority in uniform, trying to start a conversation. "Oh, um- it's been going great sir thank you." Pierre used to like Jonathan, they were in the force together for a long time, but he was beginning to feel alienated by the police force, almost as though they were antagonists in his life. The officer looked over at Xavier and quickly flashed his eyes back to Pierre. "Hey, this boy isn't giving you any trouble, is he? Can't be too careful with their lot."

As he heard those words, Pierre used all his energy to restrain himself from exploding. "No sir, Xavier is just a little friend of mine." As he looked down at Xavier, Pierre could feel the little boy shivering. Doority nodded. "Well, if we have any problems just let me know." Doority walked back to his vehicle, looking back at Xavier every now and again with suspicion in his eyes.

Pierre breathed with relief. "God, I'm so glad I don't work with these mother fuckers anymore. C'mon Xavier, let's get started with our shopping." Xavier stood rooted to where he was, a look of contempt and betrayal emitting from his eyes. "Xavier, the pig's gone, let's go."

"Why didn't you tell me you were a pig?" Pierre's heart sank. Of course, Xavier wasn't gonna react too kindly to him being part of the same force that killed his mother in cold blood. "But I'm not anymore, I promise that I've changed, Xavier!" "ONCE A PIG, ALWAYS A PIG. I THOUGHT WE WERE FRIENDS, YOU BETRAYED ME ASSHOLE." Xavier began to sprint from where he was, and without a moment's hesitation Pierre chased after him. "Please come here kid, I don't want to do anything to hurt you. I love you!" With Pierre tailing behind, Xavier finally lost breath in front of a Chinatown and collapsed to the ground in tears. Pierre patiently stood beside him.

"Those, those fucking animals took the only thing in my pathetic little life that I cared about, THEY TOOK EVERYTHING. My mom told me since I was a little child to comply with all the pig's orders, to do as they asked, no matter how absurd it was, because it's the only way you could stay safe. She was a saint, she could hurt no one, and THEY STILL GUNNED HER DOWN." Pierre nodded. "It's awful." "Let me ask you something bro, since you want to play this bullshit savior role. How many black men and women did you see gunned down in front of you, without doing jack shit about it? Nah, I bet you gunned many down yourself, didn't you? You cracker ass bitch."

On the sidewalk, Pierre took a seat next to Xavier. "Yea, you're right about me. I am a coward at best and a homicidal maniac at worst. And maybe I am desperately seeking redemption to fill that whole that's been left in my heart after all those heinous things I've done. But I promise you that I'm trying to be a different man. It may be too late now, but I want to be that brave me that my younger self would be proud of." Tears gently streaked down his eyes as Xavier began to look at Pierre again. "So, you're ready to bash some cop skulls? Stop more innocent kids from losing their mamas and papas?" Pierre began to smile. "You kidding me kid? Fuck yea I'm ready!"

***

Pierre looked at Xavier in disbelief. "We are not going to dress up in iron man and captain American costumes!" "Aww man, but I always wanted to be black Captain America!" "Look kid, if they ever make a movie about our badassery there's gonna be a shit ton of copyright issues if we wear these costumes you're proposing." Xavier sighed. "You're probably right." "Anyways, we can just wear those black masks with holes on them that burglars wear. I got a pair of them here!" Xavier shook his head. "You are the lamest." "Xavier! What we're doing isn't about looking cool and hip. We're trying to stop the pigs from fucking over innocent people. You really think Captain America or Iron Man or Batman or whatever other silly hero we idolize make it their mission to fuck up the cops?" Xavier hesitantly nodded.

"Alright, I'm gonna hand you a Beretta and a taser. Remember Xavier, we only shoot to kill if it's absolutely necessary." Xavier nodded, although Pierre was very hesitant about how sincere his nod was. "Hey bro, what about bullet proof vests?" "You're already very stealthy as it is, no need to overdo it." Anxious and jittery in their first day policing the police, Xavier and Pierre sat in an ordinary looking gray van in the middle of the city. An advanced police scanner radio sat between the two of them, alerting them for potential action.

An opportunity finally struck when it was announced on the radio that a man possibly in possession of Marijuana was nearby the vicinity of the officers. The event wasn't far from where their van was parked, so Xavier and Pierre sneakily exited their vehicles to head towards the location. As the two of them crouched down and dashed towards where the apprehension was going to be made, Xavier suddenly laughed. "You know, when I was five years old, I wanted to be an astronaut or whatever just like any other five-year boy. I never thought I was going to end up a vigilante hunting down cops with a white guy." At these remarks, Pierre burst out laughing. "Well Xavier, I suppose they were right when they told us you can do anything if you put your mind into it!"

***

Officer Jonathan Doority found the perfect opportunity to get another arrest when he saw a Blackman driving a red truck in front of him. He had little resemblance with the man they were searching for, but he was black and looked like a pothead, so it was enough. He turned on his siren as the red truck pulled over in front of a small ice cream shop. Throwing actual police procedure out the window, Doority jumped out of his police car, and instantly pointed his firearm at the truck door. "Listen carefully sir, I need you to get the fuck out of that vehicle this instant!" The man in the truck was shaking in fear as he slowly opened the door.

"Wow boy. You look spooked! In my experience, only the guilty negroes behave that way. Or maybe it's just that weed acting up!" The man shook his head. "No-no sir, I ain't got no weed,"- "SHUT UP AND GET ON YOUR KNEES." Tears of despair streamed down the man's eyes as he quickly got on his knees, but before Officer Doority could continue harassing him, someone swiftly and forcefully grabbed his neck from behind and pummeled him to the floor. It was as if a spirit had struck Doority at that moment for no man could be so surgical. As Doority got up, the man he attempted to apprehend got in his truck and drove away from the area. Pulsating with utter frustration, Doority was prepared to beat to death whoever struck him but before he had the opportunity to even identify the assailant, the space around him was empty. Doority cursed and screamed into the air. "You son of a bitch, you ain't no hero. You motherfuckers are literally letting the bad guys GET AWAY!" His knees severely damaged, Doority limped back towards his police car.

***

Over the next couple of days, there was absolute pandemonium in the city of Chataluma. More and more dirty and indecent officers were being stopped in their tracks by vigilantes attempting to hold them accountable. There wasn't even remotely a trace of who could've been responsible for these actions the city's mayor deemed "Terroristic and unpatriotic." At one point it seemed as though the culprit was finally captured while trying to stop an officer from torturing a twelve-year-old boy, but it turned out he was a copycat, merely trying to emulate the heroes who had the police shivering in fear. There was a proliferation in copycat vigilantes, making the job significantly more difficult for the police.

The mayor launched a propaganda campaign to try and win over the public, deeming these vigilantes' enemies of law and order, but it was largely ineffective, and the masses overwhelmingly seemed to support the men behind the black mask. With the police stopped in their tracks, and more ineffective than ever before, the private capital that swarmed into Chataluma began investing heavily in private security and their own police forces to keep themselves and their premises safe.

This however, only exacerbated the tension that was gripping the city as the population was rattled by the double standards in safety and protection granted to the wealthy that simply didn't exist for themselves.

***

Pierre and Xavier sat together in their small apartment room, laughing with joy as they watched the local news together. "Mannn, we got them scared shitless!" Xavier exclaimed with joy. Pierre nodded. "We sure did kid, we sure did. But you know what surprised me the most?" Xavier shook his head. "What's that?" "It surprises the fuck outta me that the people don't hate our guts." Xavier laughed. "Sure does not even those poor white Nazi crackers hating on us!" Pierre looked at the ground, a subtle inkling of shame manifesting in his eyes. "It's probably because the cops never did much protecting, spent most of our time cracking down on victimless crime and bullying innocent bystanders." Xavier looked at Pierre empathetically. "Look man, I'm not gonna glaze over reality. You fucked up bad in the past. But the shit you're doing now? It's genuinely heroic, and you've more than made up." Pierre smiled at Xaviers words. "I hope you're right. I hope God can forgive me."

True Love

Joshua looked at the headlines of the Chataluma Express newspaper with indignation and disgust as Joanna made him breakfast. "Look at this shit Joanna. These masked scoundrels are literally making it challenging for cops to get their job done!" As Joanna brought Joshua a delicious meal with scrambled eggs, bacon, and sausage, she looked at Joshua with bewilderment in her eyes. "Joshua? This doesn't sound like you at all. I mean you brought down an entire town to stick it to the big guys. You should be lauding these two vigilante types!" Joshua shook his head. "First of all, this shit isn't even remotely comparable. I was trying to protect you from that Maximillian bully and things… things unfortunately spiraled out of control. Second of all, you know what? Maybe I shouldn't have done what I did. Lots of innocent people got hurt, streets were on fire, the political establishment collapsed, I lost my fucking grandmother." Joanna gently touched Joshua's cheeks, her eyes blazing with a look of enigmatic fascination. "You're a very good man, Joshua. But I wouldn't be free to be Joanna if it weren't for you. Our love would likely be a forbidden seed that never sprouted." Joshua gently nodded.

Joanna gently kissed his lips, making Joshua blush intensely. "Hey, we should do something fun today!" Joshua nodded. "Well, I'm a pretty flexible person so hit me up! What do you wanna do?" "Well, I hear there's couples skating at the roller-skating rink today SOOO." Joshua stood up from his seat to protest. "Joanna! I don't know the first fucking thing about roller skating. We can't possibly do this!" Joanna laughed. "I thought you said you were a 'flexible' guy Joshua? Besides, I'll teach you, don't worry about it!" Joshua gazed into Joanna's eyes for a moment, uncertain of what to say. "Plzzzz, Joshua do this for me! Do this for your lover!" Joshua gently smiled and reluctantly nodded. "Okay! Okay! I'll do this dumb roller-skating thing!" Joanna glowed, despite Joshua's unenthusiastic acceptance.

***

As they entered the rink, Joshua couldn't help but notice the alarming police presence in the area. Was it always this security laden and dystopic? However, as they entered the premises Joshua couldn't help but feel as though he preferred being surrounded by the cops. Frankly, Joshua wasn't sure how to feel about what he was experiencing. There was some odd pop music in the background he couldn't quite decipher, green flashing lights he found rather irritating, and a lot...a whole lot of people. As they drew closer towards the skating rink,

Joshua began experienced a sense of terror like he had never experienced prior, and that was no hyperbole. He saw couples of all sorts, some were impossible to identify because of how androgenous they appeared, but all had one thing in common. They skated with grace and expertise.

The way their bodies moved, the way they exuded with grace and chemistry, Joshua knew he was going to humiliate himself. As Joshua stood frozen in one spot, Joanna beckoned for him to approach the rink. When it appeared as though Joshua was intent on staying rooted in place, Joanna grabbed his arms tightly and yanked him towards the rink. "Ouch! C'mon Joanna!" "Joshua, stop being a pussy and start living your life!" The moment his roller skates touched the rink, Joshua began slipping and falling all over the place. Joanna laughed hysterically as Joshua decided to rest his knees on the rink, in utter resignation. Other skaters began to notice too, and their snickers were audible from several feet away. Joanna put her arms out for Joshua to reach as the two exchanged subtle smiles at one another.

After numerous slips, falls, peculiar leg movements, and girlish screams, Joshua finally got the hang of roller skating, as he slowly but steadily began to move through the rink with grace, holding onto his lover's hands tightly. As the two gracefully moved about the rink, Joshua began to shed his arrogance. "I want to thank you Joanna, for asking me to take a leap of faith, and to venture terrains I felt uncomfortable venturing. Cuz this is really fucking nice!" Joanna flickered a soothing smile towards Joshua in appreciation. The mood began to shift significantly in the rink however as a beautiful Elvis tune began to play, one that Joshua was unfamiliar with, considering his conservative upbringing.

We're Caught in a trap I Can't Walk Out Because I Love You Too Much Baby
Joanna gently began to grab Joshua's two sweaty palms and looked intensely into his tense eyes and smiled. "I love this song."

Why Can't You See What You're Doing to Me When You Don't Believe a Word, I Say
A sense of warmth and joy began to emit inside Joshua like he'd never experienced before. "You know what babe? I think I like this song too!"

We Can't Go on Together with Suspicious Minds
"But I don't think this song captures our relationship very well!" Joanna snickered at this remark. "I love you so much Joanna." "I love you too Joshua." As the song came to a close, they exited the rink, brimming with indescribable passion and desire. Hungry, the two of them decided to visit an Italian restaurant across the street.

As Joshua sipped on the lemonade, he ordered he looked into Joanna's transfixed, glazing eyes. "I need to tell you something Joanna, something I've never told anyone before." Joanna nodded. "The truth is I don't feel like a man Joanna. I've wanted to have breasts and long hair and wear makeup my entire goddamn life." Joshua began simmering with tears, tears he kept frozen within for so long. "I hated every visit to the men's bathroom I've ever had. I felt so odd, so unnatural, so unreal." Joshua tried to wipe out the tears as they continued streaming from his eyes. "And don't get me started on the fucking showers! I can't even look down upon myself without utter revulsion." Joanna grabbed Joshua's shaking hands as tears began emitting from her eyes as well. "Yeah, those showers suck." Joshua smiled but continued. "The thing is, I don't know if I'm a woman. Maybe I'm just delusional? Or coping with my reality by constructing this alternative me?" "Let me ask you a question Joshua. Do you believe you're a woman?"

Joshua hesitated for a second and nodded. "Yes." "Well, that's all that matters Joshua! It doesn't matter if you're delusional, or coping, or some psycho mfer. You're a woman if you believe it Joshua." Joshua's body shook intensely as he hesitantly nodded. "It's just, this shit is so foreign to me Joanna, I want to understand myself but every time I inch closer to comprehension, I fall ten steps back." It seemed as though time was frozen still for a moment, but that illusion of permanent nothingness shattered as Joanna leaped from her seat across the table and gave Joshua an impassioned hug. "I know what it feels like, Joshua, to be an alien. I struck more fear into my loved one's than Satan himself." "My family was suspicious that I was a gay man for the longest time, but they refused to believe it was possible. When I revealed myself to be a trans woman, the look in their eyes was one of revulsion, indignation, and disbelief."

"My mother burst into tears, slamming her head against the glass table, drowning in despair. My father grabbed my neck tightly and slammed me to the ground. They blamed you Joshua for me opening up and finally asserting myself. They called you a blasphemous rebel sowing the seeds of moral degeneration." Listening to Joanna speak of her pain led Joshua to feel an unusual sense of appreciation for his fathers. Even his scummy father who failed to raise him and treated him like dung would never have degraded his identity in such a way as Joanna's parents displayed.

There was a moment of awkward silence, as Joshua confusedly stood rooted to where he was, unsure of what to speak next. "Hey, Joanna, could you refer to me as a she from now on?"

Joanna gently nodded. Joshua felt a sense of intense euphoria she had never experienced prior. A sort of awakening, a rebirth. But what Joshua didn't realize was that her true awakening was yet to come...

As Joanna and Joshua glowed in the mutual comfort of their presence, they were unaware that they were being overheard at the restaurant. Suddenly two men, who appeared innocent and innocuous in appearance, approached them. One wore small nerdy glasses, and had a face covered in freckles. He was pale, plump and appeared jovial. The other was skinny and looked as though he was part of some punk rock band, his hair messy and directionless. Both were wearing a suit and tie, further creating the impression of harmlessness. But the moment the two of these seemingly innocent looking men began to speak, a tense sensation began to manifest inside Joshua. "Hey ladies! Mind if we join the two of you for some dinner?" the plump one said with a suspicious pseudo friendly mannerism. Joshua was speechless but Joanna appeared confident. "Sure! We'd love to have you join us."

Smirking, the two men sat down, exuding with hubris. Joshua noticed the nerdy plump boy's hands reaching underneath the table and moments later Joanna let out a scream and jumped from her seat. The split second after Joanna let out the scream, Joshua knew exactly what happened. She got ready to jump the table and attack the two callous men, but the punk rock one suddenly pulled a firearm from underneath the table and pointed it at Joshua. "You make a single move, you fake tranny freak and I'll blow your head off." What stunned Joshua at that moment, other than the fact that a gun was pointed in her direction, was the fact that nobody in the restaurant made a move. She was certain at least a few people there carried firearms, but they simply didn't budge.

The punk rock asshole turned towards his comrade and nodded. The plump boy responded to the gesture by removing Joanna's skirt and underwear, displaying her penis to the entire restaurant. Joshua let out a horrified scream as she witnessed Joanna tearing up and shaking in utter humiliation. A crowd began to gather inside the restaurant, appearing to be more freaked out by the prospect of a girl with a penis than sexual assault. "You degenerate pervy, she male!" one man in the crowd shouted. At those words, Joshua became dizzy and collapsed to the floor, losing consciousness of everything that was happening around her. Suddenly the cynical words of her ex-history teacher began playing in her head. "Humanity was fucked. Men are pure evil." At the time, Joshua saw Charles as a depressed old man whose bleak worldview was distorted, a man who failed to see the love and sentimental beauty emitting from human nature. But at that moment, Joshua realized she was wrong.

As she regained awareness of her surroundings, Joshua

looked up and saw Joanna's dead naked body, a pool of blood surrounding her cracked face. Joshua screamed in agony. She cried and cried, resting her face on Joanna's neck. "I'm so sorry Joanna. I'm so fucking sorry. I will make them pay for this. These fucking demons. These sadistic and callous pieces of dog shit." Joshua looked up and noticed people casually going in and out of the restaurant, mothers and fathers eating with their children, as if nothing had happened. Joshua stood up and approached the front desk. "Aren't you mother fuckers going to call the cops? Somebody's lying on the floor dead! Aren't you gonna do something about that fucking shit?" The lady in the front counter shrugged. "Tranny's get beat around and die all the time. Not really worth reporting to the cops." Joshua let out a sarcastic laugh.

"Is it legal?" The lady shook her head. "Okay then call the fucking cops, or I'll kill your mother and father and if you have babies, I'll fucking kill them too you low life son of a bitch." The lady shrugged and reached for the phone, dialing 911. Joshua flinched for a moment, realizing she had never spoken that way to a person before. What was she becoming?

***

It took approximately twenty minutes, but the cops finally arrived at the scene, and Joshua, although stricken with tears and hopelessness, felt the tiny sliver of hope that justice could finally be enacted. As they entered the restaurant doors, Joshua passionately jumped towards the two officers, prepared to explain to them the callous acts of brutality she had witnessed. "Hello officers." The two men nodded at Joshua. "Where's the body?"

Joshua led the officers to the edge of the restaurant where

the naked and brutalized dead body of Joanna stood, her final look one of utter despair. The officers gazed at the body in discomfort and one of them glanced at Joshua's tormented face. "I'm sorry son, this truly must be difficult for you to grapple with." Joshua slowly nodded. "We'll examine the body and do our best to try and find this killer." Joshua noticed the officer wink and slightly grin at his colleague as he said this. "Anyways, it might take some time because in case you didn't know, our department is dealing with vigilantes attempting to break our department to shreds, so a dead pervy groomer isn't our top priority right now." At these words, Joshua began to burn inside. She was ready to leap at these men, crack their necks, and show them what true justice was. But she couldn't, she was powerless before these arbiters of law and order.

"Anyhow, we're gonna head out now, gotta catch us some criminals! I'm sorry about what you had to go through, boy." As the two officers began to head out, a thought flickered inside Joshua's fluid and disoriented mind. "Don't you guys want a description of the killers?" The two cops looked at one another with amusement. "Nah, it'll be okay! I'm sure we will find this killer without those pesky little details! Adios!" The other officer who hadn't spoken to Joshua looked at the front desk server. "Also, you might wanna clean that shit out, bad for business."

A New Deal

Flavio Luca gave a wide and ecstatic smile as he chewed on his cigar at his office at the Chataluma Iguana Casino, the largest gambling establishment in the city. He kept a torn picture of his father in front of his desk as a reminder of the torment he had to endure from inferior men drowning in mediocrity, telling him he'd amount to nothing. He could remember coming home to his father's immaculate, gold-plated home with a B- grade in mathematics and recalled the vivid horrors in his father's face. "You worthless child. I can't believe I helped birth such an idiot. You are gonna live the rest of your life cleaning toilets boy."

Yet here he was, on the verge of securing an arrangement with the cities flailing mayor, whose police force wriggled in utter terror, who's allies in big business were freaked by the grim prospects of Chatalumas economic future, and who lost all semblance of public popularity as he cut the cities programs and privatized its infrastructure. Now Flavio would not only become the most powerful living mobster in the country but secure an indestructible empire by reigning in the threat of government exposure.

Flavio gently rubbed his black beard, and with his tired black eyes, gazed into the image of his father that haunted him, with glee. He spat on the picture and laughed. "This fucking town is going to be my goddamn bitch." There was a knock at the door. "Come in," Flavio jovially stated. There entered Mayor Hellenburger, shaken to the core, and looking at Flavio in a pleading, desperate manner. "Ahhhhh, Mr. Hellenburger! Please sit down and we can begin our discussion." The mayor subtly nodded and took a seat in front of Flavio. Without hesitation, he became animated in conversation.

"Listen, I need you guys. My cops have become useless, either doing nothing or provoking ordinary citizens more intensely than ever. Capital is leaking from the city, and moving elsewhere, and these fucking commie rioters feel enabled. Then there's the goddamn vigilante scumbags trying to show the authorities who's boss! What the fuck am I supposed to do Flavio? You gotta help me!"

Flavio gave a cheery smile as the mayor shook, sweat percolating from every inch of his body. "Mr. Hellenburger, if you cooperate and work with me, I can solve all your woes! With all due respect, the mafia are men of tradition, family, and honor. We won't be busting up random blacks and latinos, pissing off the public, and causing mayhem. We will efficiently and surgically protect communities of all sorts. We will wage war on the communists. We avoided it in the past because our main worries came from the government and its goons, but with you motherfuckers off our backs we can take care of these freedom hating sons of bitches."

The stress oozing from the mayor began to progressively mitigate as Flavio spoke, a newfound sense of relief emanating in its place. "All you have to do Mr. Hellenburger, openly endorse our business as just, legitimate, and legal." The mayor took a moment to ponder the implications of such an action but ultimately sighed in resignation and nodded. "It's a deal, Flavio. But I hope you understand that we must be subtle and careful with this operation. The police can't immediately cease playing the vital strategic role it currently plays and be replaced by a group of people even more maligned and feared by the public. We need to carefully play our cards and slowly but surely hand the monopoly on violence over to the mafia."

Flavio nodded in agreement. "But Flavio, you still haven't explained to me how you'll deal with this vigilante crisis." Flavio shrugged. "You need to take care of the conditions that produce vigilantes in the first place, mayor." Dissatisfied with the answer, Hellenburger shook his head. "Fine, Flavio. I'll just take care of this shit myself."

Occupation

The sheriff of Chataluma, Steve Lewis was a stern, and gruff black man. He was supported by the political and economic establishment because his race could be utilized to dismiss critiques of systemic racism, because how could your police force be racist when it's led by a black man? The city's mayor approached the sheriff for his most brazenly bigoted plan yet, one he felt was essential to securing peace and stability.

When the mayor calls you to his own home to discuss a matter, the gravity of the subject is undoubtedly significant. Steve knocked on the red door of Mayor Hellenburgers lavish home, brimming with excitement to execute his operation. One may use the terms "Uncle Tom" or "sadistic" to describe Steve's desire to drop black blood and allow black bodies to pile up, but to Steve he was being the man his community never could be.

To Steve, black people refused to be disciplined, work hard, and act in a civilized fashion, and men like him were needed to maintain order against blackness. The community wasn't a victim, Steve thought, but rather propagated excuses to justify their failures.

***

Mayor Hellenburger answered the door and gazed into Steve's dark brown eyes in a state of glee. "My man Steve! How are you, my friend?" Steve gave a wide smile. "I'm great sir." "Very good Steve." The two men sat down in the living room, as tension began to creep in, permeating from the mayor's livid face.

"Listen, sheriff, we need to capture these scumbag vigilantes and I figure there's one way to do this." Steve nodded in curiosity. "I think it's obvious at this point that the two men responsible for scaring the cops shitless with their clown show are black men. I mean what other racial minority would feel such an intense and searing desire for justice? What other group would orchestrate such disorder and chaos?" "Sir, I absolutely agree but what do you propose?"

The look the mayor gave Steve darkened at this question. "I plan on ordering a state of emergency over this town. Its foundations are crumbling, it's morals decaying and the degenerates responsible are laughing at our incompetence. I need you Steve to concentrate police operations in predominantly black neighborhoods. Go block by block if you have to. Cut fingers, break bones, make some mother fuckers bleed. Do what we have to, to capture these freaks."

Steve smiled. "I will do this with pleasure Mr. mayor but I must insist that you feel less guilty. Believe me, I know through experience the unrelenting chaos brought forth by untamed blacks. You're doing what you need to." The mayor reluctantly nodded. "Of course, of course right sheriff. I need to toughen up! Stop internalizing these bleeding-heart liberal narratives!"

***

As the mayor declared a state of emergency, police forces, armed to the teeth, marched into poor black neighborhoods. School lessons were interrupted by gunfire and officers barged into classrooms to investigate and examine children, and staff. Restaurants and shops were closely monitored, and surrounded by armed officers, randomly harassing anyone walking down the streets.

Cops went house by house trying to ascertain information that could capture the city's number one enemy, the masked vigilantes. Desperate mothers and aunts hid their children, fearing the wrath of these little despots. It appeared as though they were hopeless and alone in the face of the oppressor.

Miles away from where all the action was concentrated, Xavier sat by Pierre in a small apartment room, despairing about their powerlessness in the face of such momentous developments. Xavier shook his head. "Man, we gotta do something about this shit dude!" "What do you want to do? Jump into the action, guns loaded and shoot all these pigs down one by one? Is that what you want Xavier? Because I'm telling you right now, that will do us no favors."

"See man, this is your white privilege speaking again. I went to these schools Pierre. I've been to many of these shops. I've met so many of these people. I have a responsibility to not just sit there and do nothing." Xavier hid his face with his hands and began to cry. "Pierre, my best friend, Donovan. The last thing I ever did was steal five dollars from him so I could buy a burger.

"And now I might never see him again." Xaviers cries of pain grew more pronounced by the minute.

Pierre sat uncomfortably, listening to Xavier. It was true that he had white privilege, that he couldn't fully comprehend the stakes and total depth of the situation unfolding. But he knew that he wasn't ready to die, and waging war on the cops was a goddamn suicide mission. Xavier stood up from where he sat and decided to assert himself. "I may die today Pierre but I'm willing to take that risk for my brothers and sisters." With those words, Xavier picked up an assortment of firearms, grabbed his mask and exited the room.

***

Sheriff Steve Lewis led a patrol of cop cars through the ghettos of Chataluma on horseback, asserting himself amidst the rubble of what he once called home. Behind the Sheriff and the vehicles that followed him were twenty black men, women and children shackled up in one row, beaten and bruised into submission prior. Five officers surrounded the perimeter, marching with the shackled black men, ready to shoot and kill if one of them attempted any funny business.

This was one of several operations throughout the city's predominantly black areas, with hundreds of black people rounded up in suspicion of conspiring to undermine the police.

There was a subtle grin emanating from the sheriff, an affirmation of his malevolent power fantasies. The picture of his lousy mother leaving him desperately starving as she purchased more and more heroin stood vividly in his mind. These people needed his dominion, needed the whip to stay in line. Of course, the sheriff couldn't be too open about how much he relished this operation, as the media was keen to portray this as an immoral, racist and unnecessary operation, and watching the sheriffs every move. As the sheriff continued to embrace his current predicament, he was interrupted by a loud noise. **BANG.**

The sound of a bullet emanated through the area, almost knocking the sheriff off his horse. There twenty feet in front of him stood Xavier. Maskless, with an assortment of firearms dangling from his waist. He was uncertain whether he would continue to hide his identity as he began his journey, but guilt ultimately rendered his decision obvious. He couldn't continue hiding behind a mask as his people were being rounded up and brutalized for his actions. As the sheriff gazed at Xavier in utter bewilderment and confusion, he spoke up. "I am the man you are looking for; I am the one who has shaken your officers to their core and left them in utter despair. It is I and only I." The sheriff sat silently on horseback for a moment. A few officers began to slowly exit their vehicles, guns drawn and ready to fire. The silence unexpectedly broke however, with a wild and roaring laughter. "Hahahaha," "Ahahahahaha. You boy? But you're just a little kid?" The other officers exchanged looks of amusement with one another.

Xavier remained stern and focused. "I will turn myself in quietly if you release my twenty brothers and sisters, and then tell your men across this city to release all the blacks they've brutalized and arrested in this egregious operation." At these words, the sheriff struggled to hold back his laughter. "Egregious? Where did you learn that fancy word son? Trying to be a white boy now, are you?" Xavier cracked a gentle smile. "You know sir, I genuinely feel quite terrible for you.

"Whatever caused you to hate your own people like this, I wish it never happened."

At these words, Sheriff Lewis lost his mind. **"SHOOT HIM! SHOOT AND KILL THIS WILD SMART-ASS NIGGA. AND THEN MURDER ALL THE CAPTIVES."** As the officers began to pull their triggers however, Xavier swiftly disappeared from his spot, leaving a series of bullets lost in midair. Losing all sense of calm, tension began to manifest the air surrounding the officers. They all began firing bullets left and right, hoping one would strike and kill the boy who confronted them. The sheriff knew this strategy would ultimately go nowhere and decided to calm his men. **"QUIT IT. QUIT FIRING YOU BOZOS. YOU'LL LOSE YOUR BULLETS AND FUCK US ALL OVER."** Slowly but surely the scene turned quiet once again.

"NOW LISTEN UP BOY. I KNOW YOU'RE SOMEWHERE OVER HERE." The sheriff mounted from his horse and approached the twenty chained black people, the confidence he exuded with prior was extinguished. He unloaded the firearm from his holster and pointed it at a small thirteen-year-old black girl who stood at the front of the line. She was shaking and tearing up, unable to comprehend what she was witnessing. Sheriff Walker smiled at her. "Aren't you a stunning beauty! Would hate to have to ruin your lovely face by putting a bullet between those gorgeous eyes!" The sheriff surveyed his surroundings. **"NOW LISTEN UP BOY. I WILL MURDER EACH AND EVERY ONE OF THESE APES IF YOU DON'T COME HERE AND FACE ME NO** *Splat.*"

Before the sheriff could continue, a bullet hit him straight between his eyes, leaving him dead on the floor. Xavier stood on top of a pine tree twenty yards away and looked at the remaining officers, an assault weapon pointed upwards and ready to fire. **"Listen you motherfuckers. Leave the innocent blacks you terrorized alone, and run away from here this instant, and none of you will have to face the wrath of my bullets."** In an instant the officers scurried from the spot like frightened rabbits. Xavier swiftly climbed down from the tree and approached the twenty poor souls chained up. The look of horror and hopelessness in their eyes left Xavier rattled, his blood boiling like it never had before. As he cut open the chains and freed them, the men, women, and children ran as if their life depended on it.

They were bruised and fucked all over, but they knew they had to escape the horrors of what they witnessed and endured. And Xavier couldn't blame them. But now that the police knew his identity, it was only a matter of time until a hoard of officers would capture him.

***

Pierre gazed at the number two hundred and thirty-four in front of him, ingrained in yellow on the door. He was on the fifth floor of his ex-wife's apartment complex and gazing into the door that led to her room. He had held back from seeing her for years, stricken by the guilt of what he had done. But his life would soon be forfeit regardless, so he thought it was an apt time to confront his uncomfortable past. Pierre knocked twice on the door. It took a few minutes, but the door opened and there stood a frail, beat down woman who Pierre could hardly recognize after all these years.

Her beautiful blonde hair and piercing green eyes continued to vibrate with the intense beauty it had years ago, but her skin was now filled with bruises, cuts, and various other maladies. She was wearing tattered pajamas and her lips were cut. Pierre gulped. "Hello Amanda." Without saying a word, Amanda led Pierre to an old and worn-out brown couch where the two sat down in a moment of absolute silence.

Amanda finally spoke up, her voice hoarse and broken down. "What the fuck do you want from me Pierre?" Pierre attempted to hold Amanda's hands, but she pulled them away. Pierre slowly began to tear up but was shut down in an instant. "This is so fucking typical of men. Tearing up and playing the victim. Why don't you use your goddamn words, Pierre?" Shaken to his core, Pierre continued to cry, pummeled by the demons of his past. "I'm so so sorry Amanda. I hit you. I degraded you. Tore you apart, piece by piece. And I know my words can never rectify my errors, but I am genuinely so sorry."

At these words, Amanda gave a tortured laugh. "You made everyone think I was a crazy, drunk bitch trying to ruin your career, motherfucker." Pierre nodded, agony overtaking his body. "The truth is Pierre; your entire existence is a facade." Pierre shook his head intensely. "No, Amanda. You're wrong. I'm a real person who makes mistakes. And I regret them with every fiber of my being." Amanda snickered. "I know it's you Pierre. You're the vigilante trying to go after these cops." Pierre sat in silence, stunned. "Want to know why I know that?"

"I know that Pierre because life is merely a sick twisted theatrical fantasy to you." Pierre began shaking more and more intensely, profusely in denial of what he was hearing. "No, you're wrong Amanda. You're wrong." Amanda smiled wider. "You know I'm right, Pierre. You didn't take up this vigilante gig because you care about social justice. You did it because you wanted to feel good about yourself, you wanted a bad ass redemption story." Pierre leaped from his couch and screamed. **"FUCK YOU AMANDA. GO BURN IN HELL YOU VILE BITCH. I'M GLAD I FUCKING BRUISED YOU, GODDAMN DELIRIOUS GOOD FOR NOTHING CUNT."**

The moment he released those words, Pierre looked at the floor in horror, unable to look his ex-wife in the face. "I'm sorry Amanda. I'm so fucking sorry." "No Pierre, you aren't sorry. You never were." Pierre began the motion of denial, shaking his head, but stopped midway. "You're right Amanda. I don't give two shits about what I've done to you. At first, I felt regretful, swimming in guilt and agony, my dreams littered with your horrified screams, leaving me broken down and drowning in a pool of self-contempt. But now, hearing you refuse my sweet and candid apology. I can't help but not give a shit anymore. In fact, I think I'm gonna murder you right here and now. That would be quite the satisfying resolution to our story, wouldn't it?"

Amanda shook her head in bewilderment. "You're even more deranged than I thought." Pierre raised his fist and struck Amanda's nose. Blood began to gush out as she attempted to run but Pierre grabbed her neck and slowly constricted her breathing, wallowing in the pleasure of her suffering. She was the villain of this story, Pierre thought to himself with conviction. She was fucking with her mind, refusing to let him be in peace with himself. As he constricted her breathing, he knew he did it out of necessity. Because pure evil shouldn't be left breathing in this universe.

In minutes, Amanda laid on the floor, dead. A pool of blood surrounded her lifeless body. Pierre gave a light sigh. "It doesn't matter if my action here was right or wrong," he whispered to himself. "Because pretty soon I'm going to die a hero."

***

Xavier hid behind a nearby bush in terror. He could hear the wailing sirens of cop cars from a distance. They would approach the proximity of the area any moment now. He could attempt to penetrate the ghettos and poor communities one by one, attempting to free all his comrades in bondage. But that wouldn't be practical. Xavier ultimately decided to confront the mayor in city hall, orchestrate a showdown that would potentially free the prisoners. But that was miles away, and Xavier needed to pass insurmountable terrains to get there undetected.

Suddenly an easily recognizable van drove towards Xavier's location, and in a split second he knew precisely what to do. Xavier shot up from the bush and waved his hands. The van stopped and he entered in a heartbeat. Xavier looked at Pierre with a smile. "So, you decided to come. Maybe I was wrong about all your crackers being trash." Pierre smiled. "So, what's the plan?" "Easy! We declare ourselves in city hall to be the vigilantes, thus forcing that crooked mayor to reverse these operations!" Pierre raised his eyebrows. "You call that easy?" "Just drive, man."

As Pierre began to speed up the vehicle, a helicopter menacingly emerged from the air, and from it emerged an officer carrying a missile launcher. Xavier screamed from the top of his lungs. **"DRIVE! FAST! WE GOTTA GET OUT OF HERE!"** He passionately pleaded. But Pierre froze at that moment, incapable of activity. The officer fired his missile launcher from the air and in a flash the van blew to shreds.

Overcoming

Joshua stood where she was, frozen in simultaneous terror and disbelief. A sensation of futile resignation began to emanate from her body, incapable of even tears. She gazed into the skating rink, where several hours ago she was having the time of her life, with the love of her life. Without putting on skates, Joshua entered the rink, walking in an absentminded fashion.

Several people nearby flickered exchanges of confusion at the sight, and few snickered and pointed at Joshua's direction. But it barely registered into her mind.

She continued to slowly walk towards the center of the rink, and when she finally reached that destination, her control dissipated, and she collapsed on her knees, breaking down into tears. Her sweaty palms began to erratically touch the floor, as if she was searching for Joanna's presence. Joshua was unaware of the dozens of people now staring at her direction. Pointing, taking pictures, and having a good laugh. The world and it's totality had become distant to Joshua, unable to escape the tortured conscience of witnessing her lover's painstakingly callous demise.

But that distance from reality faded as Joshua felt the palpable animosity of mankind surrounding him, that same animus that led to Joanna's slaughter. Joshua picked herself up from the floor and screamed in agony and disbelief. **"WHAT THE FUCK IS WRONG WITH YOU PEOPLE. HUH? WHAT THE ACTUAL FUCK IS WRONG WITH YOU? YOU SEE ONE OF YOUR FELLOW HUMANS IN AGONY AND YOU TURN IT INTO A GODDAMN SHOW?**

HUH? MY FUCKING GIRLFRIEND IS DEAD YOU KNOW THAT? YOU! YOU ALL! YOU ALL FUCKING KILLED HER."

Joshua was soaking in tears, her eyes were bloodshot, and she had lost all sense of dignity. "You all fucking killed her," she quietly whispered as the crowd continued to howl with laughter, relishing in Joshua's mad antics.

Unable to endure her predicament, Joshua dashed out of the skating rink and aimlessly ran through thousands of people, and countless streets, until she finally decided to lay down on an unoccupied bench facing a street immersed in traffic, and commerce. The dizzying sense of alienation that the dense city embodied was oddly comforting to Joshua, and as she closed her eyes, she began to more acutely comprehend her condition. "I can't just surrender." She whispered to herself. "These fucking people need to suffer for what they did to her." Joshua's brain was brimming with unpleasant thoughts that she seldom lingered upon prior. Malevolent thoughts of torture, mass execution, fiery rage embodied in unconditional annihilation. But Joshua knew she couldn't let these desires consume her, it wasn't who she was. It couldn't be.

The next day, out of a raw curiosity and desire to retrace her routes, Joshua decided to take a trip to Clairemont. She presumed that a journey to the town she supposedly liberated would give Joshua a newfound appreciation towards humanity, away from the dark, vengeful thoughts consuming every fiber of her being. Joshua decided to walk the entire terrain, desperate for the nostalgic fervor of her past, an ironic innocence that precluded her present. She walked through the forest terrain, bursting with memories, the beautiful breeze exuding with joy. This was her home in a way Chataluma could never be.

As Joshua entered the town however, the utopian image she erected on her mind was fundamentally distinct from reality. Of course, to Joshua's dismay, the grand church that overlooked the town stood erect, as proudly as ever. However, as she walked through the streets, she observed the emergence of casinos, strip clubs, gun shops, and hard liquor stores populating large swaths of the town, often nearby benign establishments such as laundromats and grocery stores.

On one particular strip, Joshua noticed a group of prostitutes huddled together, counting the meager sum of cash they had accumulated through their humiliating labor. They appeared frightened, shivering and bereft of a secure life. Men would cat call and ogle at them as they passed. Homelessness was rampant, and the way the commoners looked upon the homeless was with pure resentment and disingenuous pity. They spit and smirked at these poor creatures looking for shelter. Joshua noticed a group of teenagers stealing cash from one homeless lady carrying a sweet baby and running from the spot with glee emanating from their faces.

Joshua was yet to experience the most traumatic moment

of that trip however, the one that would reaffirm her newfound cynicism towards man. As Joshua continued to walk through the town, unrecognizable from the repressed and modest place of her childhood, she witnessed a black woman pushed around by three men, one black and two Asian. Joshua, despite the incomprehensible trauma she had experienced in the face of man's bitter wrath, couldn't hold back her altruistic instincts. "Hey. What the fuck are you doing?" Joshua exclaimed at the sight of the three men. The three men appeared confused. One of the Asian men began to protest.

"Hey look here bud. This ain't any old black bitch, it's a tranny. We doing the town a favor by keeping it away from ordinary folks!" Upon hearing those words, an unbearable realization struck Joshua, transporting her away from the present. She hadn't liberated this town. She had given the citizens a torch, an opportunity to burn the foundations and build something new and liberating. All they managed to produce was a decadent and hedonic wasteland with the same oppressive dynamics. In a flash however, the moment of contemplation dissipated, and without hesitation Joshua punched the man who made the callous remarks square on the jaw.

He collapsed instantly. The other two men who accompanied him dashed from the spot, for there was no loyalty amongst humankind. Joshua glanced at the woman she rescued for a moment, and with a curt nod began to leave. But she stopped midway and decided to say a few parting words. "Listen, I don't know who you are, but I do know that this is a sick world we live in. It's a cliche thing to say but you're either prey or predator. If I were you, I'd arm yourself and not let these wild animals take advantage of you ma'am. Remember that you know yourself better than any mfer ever could."

Continuing to shake from her tumultuous experience, the lady nodded, and Joshua dashed from the spot.

At the sight of what her town had become, Joshua's empathy for man degraded itself even further than before. She was wrong. Nothing in humanity was worth saving. It was a lost fucking cause.

Then that image of Nero she saw so long ago in her history teacher's classroom became more acute in her mind than ever before. Nero, the misunderstood emperor. The man who had enough of his species' decadent, vile, and remorseless nature. The man who became that beast of malevolent negation to destroy the foundations of evil itself. Joshua would be like him. No, Joshua would be him. She would watch Chataluma burn, just as the city made her lover burn without dropping a tear, without an inkling of mercy. But first she was gonna start with those dirty fucking cops.

***

Returning to Chataluma, Joshua took a long shower the next morning, ready to begin her spiritual quest. She had broken into some random guy's apartment room and suffocated him to death, stuffing the body in the freezer (very original). As she exited the shower however, she gazed at herself in the mirror, and realized that a significant makeover was necessary. Joshua began combing her long and messy hair, transforming it into a neat and tidy, Tom Cruise esque style. She used various creams to soften her skin, making her pale aura shine more intensely. Joshua realized she no longer could wear silly anime shirts, but instead suits and ties.

Fashionable clothing that expressed a sense of dominance and respectability.

But then, more fundamental than fashion sense itself, Joshua came to a chilling conclusion. She couldn't identify as a woman. She couldn't be who she truly was. Because who she truly was would be antithetical to the figure he would now embody. He had to repress his identity to avenge the love of his life. He had to exude with strength, and dominance and cunning womanhood simply didn't represent such characteristics in civil society. And being a trans woman would further exacerbate his mission to collapse this town, regardless of how authentic his identity truly was.

After completing his immense makeover, transforming his appearance from nerdy and uncertain to confident and clever, he laid down on "his" couch, wearing just his underwear and turned on the news channel. As he flickered through the various news channels on the television, he noticed a trend. Not merely that each channel was covering the recent exposure of the vigilantes that scared Chataluma's cops shitless, but the way each was being covered. Once the realization dawned upon the public that one of the vigilantes was a black boy, it seemed as though the iconic status they exuded with had vanished. They were now perceived as a menace to white society, and it appeared as though a significant amount of the public had flipped into supporting the police operations into black communities.

"How typical," Joshua whispered to himself. Even justice couldn't escape the blind nature of tribalism. Of course, not everyone was silent. The communists, black liberation orgs, and the black neighborhoods that were affected were up in arms. Molotov cocktails were being thrown into small businesses, streets were blocked, and several bombs placed in primarily white residencies had to be detonated. Joshua attempted to subdue the passionate anguish that filled his body as he watched the white man's twisted notion of justice. He had to act rationally and in a calculated way if he wanted to bring forth the collapse of civil society, to avenge Joanna.

Two Steps Ahead

Flavio Luca took a seat at an elegant Mexican restaurant the mayor had invited him to. It was for a crucial meeting, the mayor had insisted, about the "future" of their partnership. Flavio however wasn't a simpleton, at least not anymore. The capture of the vigilantes, the mayor's relative success in mobilizing the middle class against radical communists, and the reconsolidation of private capital at his disposal had made the mayor a more confident man than ever before. It was clear the mayor chose a public place to meet out of fear that Flavio would recklessly dispose of him upon hearing what he had to say. Upon reflecting on the circumstances and context, it was clear to Flavio that the meeting would exist as a subtle ploy to cut the mafia off.

Flavio sat impatiently; the mayor was supposed to arrive thirty minutes ago to eat dinner and discuss the plans with him. Was this a prank? An attempt to humiliate Flavio and show him who was really boss? Fortunately, the mayor eventually arrived out of a lavish limousine. He wore a distinctive blue tuxedo and was glimmering with excitement and rejuvenated energy as he entered the restaurant. He sat down across from Flavio with a subtle smile and nodded. "Hello old friend!" Flavio nodded. "Hello Mr. Mayor."

"You look quite down Flavio, is there something in particular that's bothering you?" Flavio shook his head. "No, nothing like that. Just a sleepless night. But we aren't here for a therapy session, let's get to business sir." Suddenly, the mayor burst into a fit of laughter. "Well, it brings me no pleasure in saying this Flavio, but you may require a therapy session after hearing what I must say." Flavio replied to these cocky remarks with a subtle smile. "Please, cut to the chase Mr. mayor." The mayor was flabbergasted by Flavio's demeanor. He was clearly in a tight position, as the police force had regained its confidence with the demise of the vigilantes and that should spell a curse for the dwindling mob, no?

"Well Flavio, I just wanted to inform you that I no longer need your assistance in matters. I am now a hero who took down a black radical, and we will soon see the return of law and order, this time with a passionate vengeance! I no longer require your dirty, unethical services." The mayor chuckled and winked. Flavio shook his head in disbelief, but his face continued to express a lack of genuine concern. "I had hoped Mr. Hellenburger that you'd be a more noble man. I had hoped you would reciprocate the kindness I extended towards you."
"**OH FOR CHRIST'S SAKE FLAVIO.** Grow up. You're a fossil, a relic of the past. I no longer need your service. Good day to you!" With these stern and arrogant remarks, the mayor stood up and dashed out.

Flavio snickered as he sat alone at his table. The mayor was completely unaware that Flavio had anticipated his betrayal and had a new, peculiar ally at his disposal.

Ten Hours Before Flavio Meets the Mayor

Flavio entered his lavish home and hurried upstairs towards his bedroom. He was eager to jump in bed and get a good night's rest. The day was full of skull bashing, negotiating, and political maneuvering and he needed to recharge for the next day. But much to his initial horror, somebody was already there. Flavio flickered on his bedroom lights and screamed in terror simultaneously. A fashionable man with a top hat, suit and tie, and black walking stick sat comfortably on his bed. His enigmatic black eyes pierced Flavio the moment they laid eyes on him.

Flavio reached for his holster, but the man's booming voice intervened. "Stop," he said simply and assertively, and for some odd reason Flavio simply complied with the random gentlemen's instructions. "Who the fuck are you? And what the fuck are you doing just relaxing in my goddamn bed? How the fuck did you get in here?" Flavio was stammering with an endless barrage of simple yet poignant questions. The man gracefully stood up and offered his hand to be shaken. "You can call me Nero. And I'm here as a big fan of your work, to warn you about one of your associates."

Flavio burst out laughing. "Nero? Ain't he a Greek or Roman emperor or some shit like that? What are you trying to pull here weirdo? Also, motherfucker... what in the world could you possibly know that I don't?" Nero replied with a wide, confident smile. "Roman. He's a Roman emperor." Flavio stood in place for a moment, waiting for Nero to continue, but he never did. Impatient and pissed beyond belief, Flavio shook his head, and pulled out his pistol, pointing it between Nero's two eyes. "I don't have time for this clown shit, speak or I'm gonna blow your brains out." For some odd reason he still hadn't pulled the trigger.

"You cannot trust mayor Hellenburger." Flavio smacked Nero with the butt of his firearm. "What the fuck is wrong with you? Are you trying to get me killed or something? Working for a rival mobster?" Nero rubbed the spot where he was smacked and shook his head. "No. I've been studying the current political situation extensively, and with the vigilantes wiped out, and the police force regaining its semblance of stability he's going to have no use for you. In Fact, he sees you as a hindrance." "Now hold on one second you fuckin amateur. The mayor's gotta deal with the communists, and the mob contributes to the economy, we support local communities.

"There's no way in hell he'd throw that all to the trash because some nigga and ex-cop with a white savior complex is dead."

Nero shook his head. "Your analysis is presupposing that the mayor is a rational actor, but he isn't. There's a reason you haven't shot me yet Flavio. You feel insecure, in a precarious position, and you need further validation of that justified anxiety. The mayor will dispose of you because the capitalists that puppeteer him have regained their trust in his governance when he disposed of the vigilantes. Now he will consolidate their trust by turning on the black market and further legitimizing his regime."

Flavio placed his gun back into his holster and nodded. "You're probably right but there's nothing I can do about it." Flavio slapped himself in anguish. **"I'M A FUCKING DEAD MAN."** A sinister smile began to take expression on Nero's face. "Not if you follow my plan."

The Bomb Maker

Nero sat in the Chataluma public library for hours on end, going through a swamp of books on bomb making. Unfortunately, the movies made the task appear vastly simpler than actuality. Of course, one may ponder the question of whether it was perceived as suspicious for a gentleman to go through swaths of literature on bomb making, but Nero was a master of masking his identity. He had purchased a convincing mask of an elderly bald man for his visit at the library, at a nearby magic shop, along with numerous others for a plethora of different occasions.

After skimming through what felt like the 200th book on bomb making the library offered, Nero ultimately determined that his endeavor was pointless. He would have to hire a professional bombmaker, and considering the ambitious scope of his project, it would have to be the best of the best. Nero had heard whispers of Arthur Langley, the best bomb maker in the entire nation, and although he was ecstatic and giddy at the prospect of learning bombmaking, it would clearly take significant amounts of time, something he currently didn't attain.

As Nero headed out of the library however, he was struck by a sensation of melancholy, and pitiful emptiness. The performativity of his life and its inauthenticity dawned on him like a speck of dust. He rubbed his chest in horror, realizing he had no breasts, and remembered his choice to become a man. Nero collapsed on the library floor for several minutes and squirmed at his disgusting, unreality. In moments however, he woke up to reality and dashed out of the library.

If Chataluma seemed dense and brimming with endless activity on the surface, it was nothing compared to the actual depth and endless entries and exits the city possessed. Nero had read extensively about the city for the brief period of time he had been there and ventured through dark streets and corners. On this particular occasion he was visiting the underground, a location that was deliberately difficult to reach to hinder police activity and presence. Nero entered an innocent looking coffee shop called Mama's Black Tea. Behind the tables and customers there was a black door. Behind the black door there were an additional twenty five different doors leading to a plethora of different locations.

Nero opened the red door with a cross emblazoned upon

it, and through the door was Chataluma's vibrant underbelly. The walking path was narrow and surrounded by an endless assortment of little shops, as thousands of people crammed through each other to get to their destination. The air was overwhelmed by smoke and litter, and thousands of distinct voices filled the air. Attempting to avoid trouble, Nero subtly headed for his destination. After endlessly traversing the narrow street filled with peculiar and eccentric vendors selling jewelry, owl heads, sham medicine, and the most insane shit the mind could conceive of, the street finally came to a close and became replaced with a small but dense forest area. This was where the bombmaker Nero required inhabited.

In a city rooted with immense mythology, and surreal whispers of an enigmatic past, the bombmaker was no exception. He was said to have once been a violinist for the bourgeoisie, often playing the melancholy tunes the rich fetishized with a passion. But after his family died in debt trying to pay off their cancer treatment, a more sinister side began to manifest inside the bombmaker. He bombed the limousine that carried the CEO of the health insurance company that wronged his family, and ever since he left prison, became a recluse who provided weaponry to the city's discontents.

However, the mythology was built on rumors and couldn't ever be truly confirmed. As Nero entered the cluster of trees, his eyes instantly touched upon a little cottage, and there at the front stood a man with a long white beard, beady brown eyes, and a stern pale face, intimidating, but certainly not how Nero would've expected a bombmaker to appear. The robe the man was wearing further amplified his peculiarity. Nero approached the man who gazed piercingly into his eyes, as if he was examining Nero's soul.

The man began to speak. "I have had the opportunity to experience the day-to-day lives of thousands of people. I know a punished soul when I see one and I must inform you sir that you possess the most punished of them all. So, before we proceed with business I must ask you, are you certain our transaction will bring about the satisfaction you perhaps seek?" Nero replied with a subtle nod. "I am certain sir that my business with you is the most pertinent of sorts and will cleanse my soul of its inadequacies." The man nodded and gestured for Nero to enter his cottage.

While it appeared to be an innocent, and small home from the exterior, when Nero entered the building, the illusion shattered. Somehow, against all scientific reasons, the interior was immense, with endless doors, open spaces, paintings of numerous varieties, and a massive chandelier intimidatingly looking down upon the circular area. Despite its magnificent size, the home was poorly kept and very shabby, with cobwebs and tattered furniture dominating the scene. "Come and take a seat," the bombmaker gestured towards a torn blue sofa, and the two men began the discussion.

"I need two bombs sir, one highly sophisticated and the other a generic model that can effortlessly be defused by a bomb squad." The bombmaker rubbed his beard in contemplation. "What are you planning, boy?" "One of the strings attached to the money I offer you is the absence of questions. I need you to build me a bomb so sophisticated that it would require the entire bomb squad to defuse it, and another that can be defused in a simple manner. I can offer you $200,000 for the task. $50,000 right now and $150,000 after you make the bombs. Do we have a deal?"

The bombmaker nodded. "Give me precisely five hours." Nero stood up and bowed. "I'll be back."

***

As Nero headed back to the nearby urban cluster of Chatalumas underground, he decided to visit a local sushi shop; it had been ages since his taste buds had experienced the raw wonders of sushi. As he opened the wooden gate to the restaurant however his eyes flashed to a bar thirty feet away surrounded by protesters. They overwhelmingly appeared to be white men flashing the Crucifix towards the front of the bar as a group of women screamed at them to cease their antics. One man appeared to throw a Molotov cocktail at the glass and another a stone. Nero looked at the wooden door he was about to enter and sighed. The sushi would have to wait.

Nero removed his pistol for its holster and approached the mob descending upon the bar. Without hesitation he shot his gun in the air and asserted himself with conviction. **"CEASE IMMEDIATELY."** In an instant, the mob went silent and turned towards Nero. One of the men replied with disbelief. "Look sir, imma assume you're a good man, considering the fact that you a gun owner, and it's always heroic and stuff to stand up for what's right. But what we have in that bar ain't no ordinary people. They a bunch of lousy, no good faggots." Nero struggled to maintain his composure. After all, he was no longer Joshua, but instead a cold, calculated and calm destroyer. But it wasn't easy to keep calm in the face of such unabashed bigotry.

Nero smiled and nodded with disingenuous amusement. "Oh, well, if they're just a bunch of faggots, go on with your endeavor." The men continued with their assault upon the queer bar, chanting "burn in hell sodomite" as they spit and attacked the bars infrastructure, some with axes and maces.

Nero furiously dashed towards a gas station a few yards across the bar and quickly purchased a liter of gas. As he hurriedly ran back to the bar under assault, he witnessed dozens of men, women, and other sexual minorities rushing up against the crusaders to protect their place of comradery. Seeing these helpless people using every fiber of their being to fight back against zealots, shoving, kicking, biting, and smashing their way against these freaks with every object they could find, inspired Nero to rush into the crowd of bigots and dump gasoline all over them.

The senseless men, who had already shamelessly beaten several queers to a pulp and laid havoc to the establishment stopped what they did and looked at Nero with astonishment. Before they could react further, a flicker of flames emitted from Nero's lighter, as he threw it into the gasoline, a massive fire erupting where the theocratic menace stood. The prideful men suddenly lost their gleeful and brazenly destructive demeanor and ran for their lives. The flames were particularly vicious for the men at the center who were engulfed in flames, screaming in utter revulsion, many of their fellow bigots abandoning them.

Through the flames however, Nero observed the eyes of numerous people, black, Hispanic, Asian, indigenous, Indian, and various other ethnicities, all queer, glowing with both shock and a reluctant appreciation. Nero hesitantly approached them as a black man who appeared slender, bald and youthful ran towards Nero. Expecting a warm greeting, what Nero received instead was a slap in the face. "Heyyyy man, what the fuck do you think you're doing?" Nero was alarmed by the physical gesture and remarks. "What the fuck do you mean? I assisted you guys against those loons!" The man looked down at the sidewalk and shook his head. "Nah, you can't just light a fire and watch these crackers blaze away into their piece of shit grandmother's basements. What you did has consequences. They're gonna return, more pissed off than ever and possibly try to shoot us all dead." Nero nodded in resignation. "I apologize, I thought I was doing a positive service but clearly my behavior was reckless and ill conceived." The man raised an eyebrow. "Wow, you're the first cracker I've met who didn't get all up in my face for basic criticism. What's your name son?" Nero looked into the starry night sky, fogged by the smoky residues of industry, with emptiness all over his face. "I don't know what my name is."

The man's response to Nero's peculiar answer surprised him immensely. "That's all right! Figuring out our identities and how we want to express them can be a challenging and arduous process!" The two men stood together in silence for a moment. "My name is Jackson by the way. Would you like to head to our gay little bar and have a nice cold beer with me?" At that moment, Nero snapped. He slapped the man in the face as aggressively as possible, with all his might and energy, and dashed from the spot. The man didn't bother to follow him, but Nero continued to run as far away from the scene as he could.

He was no longer Joshua, he was Nero. He couldn't let the kindness and warmth of man turn him back into that naive little brat who saw sunshines and rainbows. Man was cruel, man was torturous. Man was a vile and pestilent being with no regard for those around him. Nero couldn't indulge in the illusions of love and empathy and joy that man maliciously emitted. He had seen with his eyes what they had done to his love. Gleefully humiliating her as she begged with all her might for pity, for forgiveness, for compassion, till she fell to the floor, dead, with a pool of blood. Nero screamed in agony into the streets. They were filled with people and commerce and conversations, but to Nero it was an empty barrage of spectacular distractions, confronting him as an enemy.

He had allowed some foolish and altruistic side quest at the bar distract him from his mission of watching Chataluma burn, and avenging the love of his life, and he hurriedly rushed back to the bombmaker who was supposed to have completed the task by now. As Nero once again entered the premises of the bomb makers seemingly humble but extraordinary cottage, he saw the man appear frightful, and exhausted, as he thrusted a large suitcase towards Nero. "I have built the bombs for you and placed them in this suitcase. I must warn you however to not tamper with things beyond your reach, to not disturb the vibrant and stable world our god designed." Nero rolled his eyes. "If you're so concerned with peace and stability old man, why the fuck do you build bombs for people?"

Nero noticed a gentle teardrop from the bombmaker's eyes. "I accepted ages ago, son, that I would rot in hell. I long for the day that some punk drops in and shoots me in the head. At Least I would know then that a creator looks over us with his benevolent will." Nero looked at the man with pity. "There is no god, there is just a cruel world with cruel beings and cruel intentions. Stop latching onto these pitiful illusions and wake the fuck up. That's my advice to you bud." Nero left the scene, rubbing the tears from his eyes, the vulnerable tears he hid away from the bombmaker.

Nero had chosen his path.

Choice

Nero watched the television in amusement as Chatalumas arrogant mayor paraded the streets, with millions of imbeciles cheering him on, seemingly indifferent to the fact that he cut healthcare, food stamps, and all the programs the desperate needed to keep living fruitful lives. The news footage of course had conveniently cut out the hundreds of thousands of protesters across the city, burning and looting stores, and attempting to penetrate the kabuki theater on display.

Nero found amusement at the idea that the gleeful mayor would soon experience a nightmare more ruthless than anything the greatest horror writers could conjure up. Nero picked up his suitcase, and headed out to his first destination. The area was relatively small in size, with a huge, concentrated population of impoverished Caucasians living together in broken down cabins and poorly maintained apartment complexes. These were poor men and women who refused to live with racial minorities and preferred experiencing their poverty in a racially homogenous part of the city, largely ignored by the city's bustling elite.

As he walked towards his specific destination, Nero couldn't help but grimace at the sight of his surroundings. Skinny and malnourished little girls were dashing out of convenience stores with stolen cans of soup. At every corner, the homeless stood with empty cans in front of them, begging for pennies. At one corner near the dumpster, Nero noticed an aged man, biting into the raw flesh of a dead dog, chewing the meat with bitter revulsion and desperation in his eyes.

Nero was about to vomit as he finally reached his destination, Harrison Elementary School, at the outskirts of Chataluma. This was where Caucasians in extreme poverty often took their children to get a meager and barely serviceable education, to read, write, and count to hundred if they were lucky.

Nero stood in the front steps of the school for a moment, taking in the immense gravity of what he was about to do. It would've been entirely unfathomable to Joshua, reprehensible to the highest degree imaginable. But Nero knew it was for the greater good. The school was in tatters like the rest of the outskirts, the glass shattered in many locations, the paint job lazily done. The school was one story in size, without a playground, and just one tiny cafeteria for the kids to eat their lunch. The security for the school were volunteer parents who knew the police had abandoned them and were left to protect their children. Nero didn't have to concern himself with security however, as Flavio Luca's men had eliminated that issue with ease.

The school hallways were quiet as Nero entered, the children were likely engaged in class. One young girl had left her classroom to use the bathroom, and looked at Nero with an expression of concern as he walked past her. Nero entered the teachers' lounge, a little area where the teachers sat down to chat and eat their lunches. The room was empty, as Nero anticipated and he sat down and opened his suitcase. He picked up the small bomb, easy to diffuse, and placed it underneath a table. It would take mere minutes for the bomb squad to deal with the threat if given the opportunity to act. There were thousands of students cramped into this building, and as Nero set the bomb to be detonated in one hour, he knew these children would perish before the eyes of a morally bankrupt government.

Of course, the plan was for somebody to find the bomb in precisely twenty minutes, and Nero had paid someone heftily for just that task. He had accrued immense wealth from the man he murdered and stole the apartment room from, something he would use to his advantage. As he began to exit the building, Nero could hear the little boys and girls sing a nursery rhyme in their classrooms, a tinge of guilt emanating from his heart. But all those kisses, dances, anniversaries, little moments he could've had with the woman he loved, that were ruthlessly stolen from Joshua, allowed him to overcome his guilt as he left the school.

The second bomb Nero had to place and detonate would be far more challenging, but without the same sensations of guilt and inner decay. Nero had dressed for the occasion, with a flamboyant suit and tie, to blend in with the bourgeois he would soon rub shoulders with. Nero was headed to the southern part of Chataluma, where the wealthy and upstanding members of society resided, far from the noisy and decadent masses. Major oil executives were holding a party at the Grand Prix Hotel, a very lavish five-star hotel, pink in the exterior, with rooms and decorations emanating with gold and silver inside. Flavio had his men bribe the security outside with impressive sums of cash to allow Nero entry into the hotel, however refused to act further, in fear that he would alienate the city's elite if he was found to be complicit in what was to come.

As Nero entered the building with his suitcase, he couldn't help but appreciate the stark contrast between the two parts of Chataluma he had experienced. There were no raw dogs being eaten or broken pipes and worn-down paint. There were exquisite lifestyles brimming at every moment. Men drinking champagne, flirting with every female employee they could get a hold off, engaged in peculiar ceremonial esque dances. Nero attempted to avoid detection as he headed for the hotel's laundry room, but was stopped in his tracks moments after he entered the building.

A stern looking Asian officer approached Nero with suspicion written across his eyes. "Sir, before you go further, I would like to see what materials you possess in that suitcase of yours." Nero raised his eyebrow. "You are just a commoner, a filthy little cog in this machine my billion-dollar company owns. I can have you fired, little man." Nero could feel the turmoil the officer was experiencing within himself. A dialectical struggle between the desire to retort and fend off against the humiliating remarks Nero made and the desire to conform and obey so he can keep his job as an officer. Ultimately the ladder won out, and the man nodded his head with frustration. "My apologies sir, please feel free to move forward."

As Nero narrowly passed that obstacle, he noticed the clearly drunk executives were now wearing masks and fondling each other in pleasure. The hypocrisy of what he witnessed made Nero want to explode with fumes. These men all promoted public decency and puritanical measures aimed at suppressing and repressing sexual minorities, and yet here they were engaged in the same activities that would've gotten anyone killed for displaying. Nero couldn't be distracted however from such brazen displays of irreconcilable moral contradiction, and headed for the laundry room. There was a sign at the front that said the laundry room was "under maintenance and not safe to enter," however, Nero had paid an employee to place that sign there so he could proceed with his plans.

As he entered the laundry room, Nero once again opened his suitcase and pulled out a far more sophisticated bomb that would require an entire bomb squad to diffuse. It was composed of numerous convoluted blue and red wires moving in a variety of distinctive directions. Nero simply placed the bomb at the floor of the laundry mat, setting it to detonate in forty-five minutes, and headed out of the room. In moments, a man was expected to come and announce the existence of the bomb. Nero exited the hotel from the back, a sinister smile overtaking his wary face.

***

Mayor Hellenburger sat rooted to his chair in terror. He reread the letter in front of him over and over, agonizing over every detail. This had to be a malicious prank right? It couldn't possibly be real? He was forced to make the most difficult choice in his career, a choice between thousands of poor students whose parents likely couldn't donate a nickel to his campaign, and a couple of billionaire oil executives who were essential to his campaign. According to the letter, the bomb located in the Grand Prix Hotel required every member of the bomb squad to successfully detonate, not a single member could assist the school. Of course, if the executives tried to evacuate it wouldn't make a difference because of the bombs range.

Letters were distributed to several government officials, informing them of this choice. If this wasn't a prank, it would leak to the entire media that Mayor Hellenburger chose a couple of oil executives over thousands of dead children. "But the negative press would fade away," the mayor assured himself. "I can just call their parents welfare leeches to the public and they'll buy it," Hellenburger whispered to himself. After moments of consideration and calculation, the mayor finally made his decision. "Send the entire bomb squad to the Grand Prix hotel!" the Mayor reluctantly exclaimed. If hell existed the mayor had already sealed his fate from years of sinful activity, why bother changing now?

Much to his despair, the mayor received a call from the bomb squad, confirming his worst fears. It wasn't a silly prank, there was a bomb on the verge of being detonated in the Grand Prix Hotel. The mayor took out his notebook and began preparing talking points to mitigate the blow that would inevitably derive from thousands of students burning to crisps, because of his inaction. "These oil executives brought millions of jobs to the city, they were necessary to keep this city from economically plummeting," the Mayor jotted down in his notebook. As the mayor jotted down numerous ideas to save face from the incoming cataclysm that would plague the city, his phone rang again to send a more hopeful message.

"We have successfully defused the bomb," the squad leader extatically announced to the mayor. The mayor's heart began to relax a moment after digesting the news from the bomb squad. Perhaps there was no bomb in Chataluma's outskirts. Who would wanna bomb some kids in a shithole nobody cares about anyways? Perhaps the mayor would be declared a hero to the entire city for saving numerous elite lives! The mayor's wishful thinking however, instantly evaporated with a **BOOOOM**. The explosion from the outskirts was so incomprehensibly loud it was heard from virtually every corner of the city and beyond. As the noise vibrated to his apartment room, Nero danced to Beethoven's Ode to Joy. Flavio sat in his mansion, chewing on a cigar. His heart was beating fast, because he broke a moral barrier he had never broken before. He assisted in massacring children. But to ascend to power, one often had to transgress boundaries.

News of the deadliest bombing in Chataluma's history spread like wildfire throughout every corner of the city. At first, millions mourned, holding vigils, and ceremonies to honor the slain victims. The city had gone quiet, losing its restless nature for a few moments. Flavio visited the site of the bombing in agony, and placed a rose at the front of the now collapsed school building. However, much to the mayor and city elites dismay, the peace and calm dissipated quickly. It started with one or two restless men attempting to barge into city hall, but within moments became a movement of hundreds of thousands of outraged citizens, unable to fathom the news that was emerging around the event. You could hear the cries of disbelief expressed in the streets. "The mayor just let 'em die even though he got a motherfucking letter warning him about this shit?" Nero heard an indignant lady scream in disbelief as he strolled through the city.

The tense situation only escalated for the worse as time progressed, and soon the oil executives whose lives were saved by the mayor had their houses stormed and looted as they ran as far away from the city as possible. There was never a moment in history so magnificent since the storming of the Bastille as men, and women brought buildings to flames, and partied on the ashes of decimated homes, casually popping out bottles of champagne and dance music as they broke through wealthy neighborhood after neighborhood, tearing through the security apparatus with ease.

Unfortunately, the mayor was not a politically astute man, in fact he was a brainless and out of touch git, and he brought about his undoing just as he attempted to ease the situation. The mayor held a rally several days after the terrorist attack unfolded, and decided he would try out the talking points he had written down as the catastrophic event had unfolded. What the mayor didn't realize however, was that the victims of his malicious incompetence were white this time around and thus mattered more in the eyes of the white majority. Before he could begin to express himself on stage, three gunmen approached the podium and in moments, Hellenburgers body laid on the floor, sprayed with bullets, in a puddle of blood. The men who assassinated him were never captured.

Flavio Luca was the king of Chataluma.

Betrayal

Two of Chatalumas most talented professional hit men stood in front of Flavio Luca. Luca should've felt a rejuvenating sense of strength and passion since the school bombing that left the city in his fingertips, but instead it left him in a state of irreconcilable guilt. And he knew just who he needed to kill to assuage that feeling. Of course, he couldn't publicly expose Nero; since he was complicit in the act, he too would ultimately be brought down. So instead, he decided to wipe out the threat in a more subtle fashion.

When Luca gave the hitmen a description of how Nero appeared and his mannerisms however, he failed to realize two fundamental things. Firstly, Nero was a showman. He changed his appearances and mannerisms in whatever way was convenient at the moment. Secondly, perhaps more critically, he knew Flavio well enough to know he'd stab him in the back the moment he was given the opportunity. So, Nero already paid off the city's professional hitmen to inform him when Flavio had given the order to take him out.

The moment he was informed that Flavio had given out the order to take him out, he knew it was time to retaliate. But Nero wasn't interested in simply killing Flavio, that would be too simple of a task. To truly bring the city to its death kneel, he would have to murder Flavio in such a way that he collapses all hierarchy and structure within the mob world, bringing it into a perpetual state of war. Then the city would be cleansed of its order, and shattered to its core.

As far as mobsters went, Flavio was a clever man. The moment the wealthy, police, and government were overrun by mobs of angry men and women, unsettled by the casualties their rulers left in their wake, Flavio set the grounds for a fair capitalist economy. He offered security for people across the city for cheap prices, with far greater reliability than the dirty cops, infamous for their bigotry and laziness, offered. He threatened companies that refused to pay fair wages to their employees and declared massive investments to assist the poor and working class. His attempts at constructing a more fair capitalism undermined the legitimacy of the communists, and the remaining radicals were crushed under his boot.

But Flavio had a glaring weakness that could be exploited to Nero's advantage. Nero couldn't quite put his fingers upon it yet, but he knew it was deeper than most people realized. Of course, it was commonly known that Flavio had an obsession with impressing his now dead father (likely murdered by Flavio), who he simultaneously despised with all his passion and yet constantly attempted to live up to. But Nero could feel a deep-seated pain in Flavio's eyes, the experience one felt when they lost someone, they truly loved and cherished; an experience Nero understood only too well. To further investigate the situation, Nero decided to visit the part of Chataluma Flavio had grown up in, perhaps there he would find the answers required to put the puzzle pieces together.

There was a heavy Irish and Italian presence in the Northeastern part of Chataluma. It was a humble area, very distinct from the boisterous, noisy, impersonal, alienating and often callous attributes that defined the rest of the city. The Autumn leaves were crisp orange and the sun shone with clarity as Nero strolled the suburbs, uncertain of what precise step to take next. He ultimately decided to visit the library nearby the area. Perhaps a library so close to the proximity of a major social figure would provide relevant information. As expected, there were numerous novels, accounts, and stories scattered throughout the library detailing the adventures and life of Flavio Luca, but none provided the critical information Nero required. It was nonetheless difficult to read about Luca's childhood, as detailed accounts were written about the excruciating and borderline torturous treatment he received at the hands of his father.

He was burnt with matches, hit with paddles, and verbally taunted for never living up to his family's absurd expectations. Seeing such vivid descriptions of callous parenting made Nero slightly grateful to have a father who might've been shitty but never imposed cruel expectations upon him. As Nero exhaustively went through numerous books on the subject of Flavio Luca, he finally decided to toss his hat in resignation and sighed heavily. Clearly this wasn't going anywhere.

As Nero dashed out of the library, he couldn't help but observe a sensation of unfulfilled longing in the suburban landscape that confronted him. It was fetishized by the middle class as an ideal to achieve. To live free from the torments of the city with a wife, nice house, picket fence, dog, and children. But it exuded an empty solitude, an isolation from social relations and atomization that forced the fragile human ego to traverse a terrain they could hardly escape.

Perhaps this suburban hellscape was where Flavio was pounded to submission, forced to reproduce the ideal life his parents had built, shredding every inch of the poor child's dignity as he struggled to make sense of his oppressive condition. But perhaps it was mere speculation on Nero's part. Nero, mindlessly drifting through another man's birthplace, decided upon visiting the cemetery. He always had a fascination for the lands where the dead were buried, the way it was zoned off from the rest of society like a menacing plague only visited by those haunted by man's greatest nightmare, loss.

All the regret, lost hope, memories of an incomprehensible condition, were underneath tombstones, relishing in its escape from the torments of unfulfilled life. Nero observed each and every tombstone he walked past as his mind scurried for the critical detail that would allow him to unleash unforetold misery upon the city. As he traversed the land of the dead, Nero observed an elderly woman a couple feet in front of him. She gazed transfixed into a tombstone that took the shape of a bent cross. On the tombstone read the name "Mary Elizabeth Hamilton."

The lady didn't make a single miniscule movement as Nero approached her direction, but she began to speak. "I come here every single day darling, to be with my daughter. I know she speaks to me from the heavens, she sings lullabies that only my ears can take in." Nero gave a warm smile in response. "I'm sorry for your loss ma'am, I hope she is thriving in the heavens.

I've lost family too, you know. It's a burdensome process to recover from." The lady finally made a movement as her tired green eyes gazed at Nero. "You haven't lost love like I have boy. I can promise you that."

Nero touched his lip for a moment and spoke. "Don't assume things about people you don't know ma'am. I watched as the love of my life was beaten to a pulp, ruthlessly executed, as crowds of people laughed at the sight of her discomfort." The old woman grabbed Nero's shoulder. "Would you like to come over and have a cup of coffee with me? We can chat a little bit more if you'd like." Nero gazed into the writing on the gravestone underneath the name.

Sloppily written underneath Mary Elizabeth Hamilton were the words "To Love Is to Sacrifice." After a moment of contemplation, Nero nodded to the old lady's request. "I would love to have a cup of coffee with you."

***

Nero looked around the gracious old woman's little one-story home. Every wall was dominated by pictures of the same girl, at various ages and points of her life. In some pictures she wore blue, red, and green dresses; in others jeans, sweatpants, and shirts of numerous varieties. It didn't take a detective to deduce who these pictures depicted. Mary Elizabeth Hamilton was a pale girl, with a glistening smile and piercing blue eyes, as grandiose as the ocean itself. She had the most magnificent blonde hair. Mary wasn't particularly tall, perhaps 5' 6" at most.

As the elderly woman poured Nero a cup of coffee, he couldn't help but speak words of remorse. "I'm sorry about what happened to Ms. Hamilton, she must've been an incredible woman." The woman comfortably took a seat next to Nero and nodded. "She was God's most gracious creature. Humble, sweet, always offering a helping hand to those who needed it. But most of all, she was mine." Nero gave a warm and understanding smile.

"You know, part of me wishes she was a bratty little bitch. A completely unlovable asshole. Because then perhaps she'd still…she'd still be with me." The woman broke down in tears with these words, laying her face against the kitchen granite. "Those beasts had to decimate all the beauty and wonder in this world. **MY BEAUTY. MY WONDER.**" Nero looked guiltily into his cup of coffee. Feeling a sense of profound humiliation for being human.

Much to Nero's amazement, the broken-down woman regained her composure and began to recount a story. "My sunshine, my light in this world. She was the happiest she had ever been before her life was so mercilessly stolen from her." Nero held back tears as the lady began to tell her story, for the more she spoke, the more Nero could painfully relate to his own bitter memories. "Mary had met the love of her life. I had supported her enthusiastically because the boy was part of a wealthy family, an elite family. The boy's name was Flavio Luca." Nero nearly spit the coffee from his mouth at the sound of that name. The lady continued to speak, ignorant of his reaction.

"Flavio and Mary loved each other so much, you wouldn't believe it. Every day, Mary would come back from school, blushing and smiling uncontrollably. He was all she could ever think of at the time, and she was all he could think of. But Flavio's parents weren't too fond of the arrangement, his bitter father in particular. He thought my daughter was a good for nothing whore and gold digger exploiting Flavio for wealth. He often mocked Flavio and pushed him around for falling in love with my daughter. He thought my daughter was the fucking devil incarnate! Why? Because she was a good for nothing waitress with an unemployed mother of course!"

"Eventually, Flavio and Mary met more often in private, away from the judgmental eyes of his father. I oversaw them on top of an apple tree once, biting the same fruit together, whispering together about their future, what they'd name their child if they ever- if they ever," Mary's mother couldn't finish the sentence as she broke down in tears once again. Nero reached out his arms in an effort to comfort her, but she slapped them away. She swiftly wiped away her tears and continued to speak.

"His father decided to take matters into his own hands. He informed Mary and Flavio that he accepted their love and adoration for each other, and to celebrate, asked the two of them to join him for a hiking trip. Mary, an enthusiast for the natural world herself, accepted the invitation. And let's just say... let's just say her body was never found again." This time it wasn't merely the broken mother who burst into tears. Nero cried with her. He reached across the kitchen table and hugged her tightly. His eyes were redder than the sun, he had never cried so intensely, with such vigor and aimless agony.

"I am so sorry miss."

Awakenings

Nero now had at his disposal the ability to bring the mob world into turmoil, to see the city engulfed in flames as he had desired. He could easily dress up as Mary and fool Flavio into believing he was a spirit from the past. Love intoxicates people in that way. He could manage to get Flavio to do anything. But Nero was broken. He realized more clearly than ever that watching the world burn to ashes would never satisfy him. Nero needed the touch of a lover to live out his final moments, not the false satisfaction of watching the world collapse before his eyes. That's how he could truly honor Joanna.

But it was time to stop living a fictitious life. "I'm not a man." Nero whispered to herself in the mirror. "I am proudly a woman, and I am proudly a tranny like my father before me." Nero removed her articles of clothing, never quite comfortable with the suits, and sweatpants she wore. Nero put on a vivid and magnificent red dress she found while shopping at the nearby mall, put on some red lipstick, and powder on her cheeks. Before leaving this world for good however, she had one final task.

***

Flavio Luca sat timidly on his living room couch. The room was lit red with a painting of magnificent horses piercing the night sky at its center. He had become the man his father said he could never become, yet he felt sheer emptiness. As if his father sat perched in his mind like an inescapable nightmare gnawing away at his bitter existence. Whether it was a hallucination, or a real-life experience, Flavio would never know, but suddenly a breathtaking woman appeared in front of him, with a red dress, very poorly done makeup, and short hair.

Flavio sat back in awe. He wasn't aware that drinking whisky produced such vivid depictions of feminine beauty. The woman began to whisper the same three words over and over again.

"You Are Enough." "You Are Enough." "You Are Enough."

Flavio put his hands in his face as he embarrassedly burst into tears. Those three words pierced his heart in a way that no words ever had before. It was the words his father would rather kill himself than whisper to his inadequate son. As Flavio's tears melted, he finally mustered the courage to look up once again. Nothing appeared in front of him.

***

Nero stood atop the tallest skyscraper in Chataluma. She could see the entire city in its magnificent aura in front of her. Her red dress blew against the wind, as she gazed in awe at God's creation. Only when one looks deep into the abyss of nothingness and all its intricate design, do they touch the soul of divinity. The city was engulfed in flames, men, women, and children fighting to survive with every inch of their being. But nature had a way of healing.

Nero looked up into the night sky and smiled at the moon as its vibrant light penetrated her anxious face. Tears of remorse and understanding swelled up in her eyes as her heartbeat with passionate cravings. She would be with her lover. And her long-lost father soon enough. She would be with Charlie. She would be with the thousands of souls she plunged into the depths of the netherworld.

Nero shut her eyes and jumped.

Epilogue

Flavio Luca shut down his mob operations with little hesitation after his visit with the lady in the red dress. He became a recluse, spending the rest of his days in the mountain side, painting the most exquisite and fiery portraits of his lost love. Of course, the wounds inflicted upon him by his loathsome father never fully healed, but stood as a reminder of the man Flavio could never become.

Chataluma's appetite for violence and decay eroded, with men and women sick and tired of losing their children to the mercy of a decadent and narcissistic culture of materialism and unaddressed fear.

The cause of the strife, violence, and chaos inflicted upon the city by its own creation was never known. Nero was lost in the vastness of time, a puppeteer of chaos in an enigmatic period. Her name merely a fable taught to children for centuries to come, a warning to societies retreating from compassion.